SMALL CHANGE

SMALL CHANGE

a collection of stories YEHUDIT HENDEL

BRANDEIS UNIVERSITY PRESS

Published by University Press of New England

Hanover and London

Brandeis University Press
Published by University Press of New England
One Court St., Lebanon, NH 03766

Published by arrangement with
The Institute for the Translation of Hebrew Literature
Originally published in Hebrew by Hakibbutz Hameuhad, Tel Aviv,
in *Kesef Katan* (1988) and *Aruhat Boker Tmima* (1996)
Foreword by Lily Rattok © 2002 Lily Rattok

This project has received support from the National Endowment for the Arts and the
Jacob and Libby Goodman Institute for the Study of Zionism and Israel.

Printed in the United States of America

5 4 3 2 1

Library of Congress Cataloging-in-Publication Data
Hendel, Yehudit.
[Short stories. English. Selections]
Small change : a collection of stories / Yehudit Hendel.
    p.cm. — (The Tauber Institute for the Study of European Jewry series)
Contents: Story with no address / translation by Barbara Harshav—The
letter that came in time / translation by Marsha Pomeranz—My friend B's
feast / translation by Dalya Bilu—Low, close to the floor / translation by
Dalya Bilu—Small change / translation by Dalya Bilu—Fata morgana
across the street / translation by Dalya Bilu—Apples in honey / translation
by Barbara Harshav—Late revenge / translation by Barbara Harshav.
ISBN 1-58465-279-9 (alk. paper)
1. Hendel, Yehudit–Translations into English. I. Harshav, Barbara,
1940– . II. Pomeranz, Marsha. III. Bilu, Dalya. IV. Title. V. Series.
PJ5054.H454A24 2002
892.4'36—dc21   2002013291

"Small Change" originally appeared in *Six Israeli Novellas,* Gershon Shaked, ed. First
edition published by David R. Godine, Publisher, 1999, second edition to be published
by David R. Godine in 2003. Copyright © 1999 by the Institute for the Translation of
Hebrew Literature.

ACKNOWLEDGMENTS

"A Story with No Address": English translation by Barbara Harshav first published in *Delos,* vol. 2, no. 1, spring 1989 College Park, Md., 1989; also in *The Oxford Book of Hebrew Short Stories,* ed. G. Abramson, Oxford: Oxford University Press, 1996, and in translation, in the *Journal of Literary Translations,* New York, 1993. Copyright © Barbara Harshav.

"The Letter That Came in Time": English translation by Marsha Pomeranz first published in *Stories from Women Writers of Israel,* New Delhi: Star, 1995. Copyright © The Institute for the Translation of Hebrew Literature.

"My Friend B's Feast": English translation by Dalya Bilu first published in *New Women's Writing from Israel,* ed. Risa Domb, Ilford: Vallentine Mitchell, 1996. Copyright © The Institute for the Translation of Hebrew Literature.

"Low, Close to the Floor": English translation by Dalya Bilu first published in *The Jewish Quarterly,* no. 132 (1988–89); also in *A Married Woman and Other Short Stories,* New Delhi: Star, 1995. Copyright © The Institute for the Translation of Hebrew Literature.

"Small Change": English translation by Dalya Bilu first published in *Six Israeli Novellas,* ed. G. Shaked, Boston: Godine, 1999. Copyright © The Institute for the Translation of Hebrew Literature.

"Fata Morgana across the Street": English translation by Dalya Bilu first published in *Modern Hebrew Literature,* No. 18, 1997; also in *Not Just Milk and Honey,* ed. H. Hoffman, New Delhi: National Book Trust, 1998. Copyright © The Institute for the Translation of Hebrew Literature.

"Apples in Honey": English translation by Barbara Harshav first published in *Ribcage,* New York: Hadassah, 1994. Copyright © Barbara Harshav.

"Late Revenge": English translation by Barbara Harshav. Copyright © The Institute for the Translation of Hebrew Literature.

THE TAUBER INSTITUTE FOR THE STUDY OF EUROPEAN JEWRY SERIES

JEHUDA REINHARZ, General Editor
SYLVIA FUKS FRIED, Associate Editor

The Tauber Institute for the Study of European Jewry, established by a gift to Brandeis University from Dr. Laszlo N. Tauber, is dedicated to the memory of the victims of Nazi persecutions between 1933 and 1945. The Institute seeks to study the history and culture of European Jewry in the modern period. The Institute has a special interest in studying the causes, nature, and consequences of the European Jewish catastrophe within the contexts of modern European diplomatic, intellectual, political, and social history.

The Jacob and Libby Goodman Institute for the Study of Zionism and Israel was founded through a gift to Brandeis University by Mrs. Libby Goodman and is organized under the auspices of the Tauber Institute. The Goodman Institute seeks to promote an understanding of the historical and ideological development of the Zionist movement, and the history, society, and culture of the State of Israel.

Frances Malino and Bernard Wasserstein, 1985
The Jews in Modern France

Jehuda Reinharz and Walter Schatzberg, editors, 1985
The Jewish Response to German Culture: From the Enlightenment to the Second World War

Jacob Katz
The Darker Side of Genius: Richard Wagner's Anti-Semitism

Jehuda Reinharz, editor, 1987
Living with Antisemitism: Modern Jewish Responses

Michael R. Marrus, 1987
The Holocaust in History

Paul Mendes-Flohr, editor, 1987
The Philosophy of Franz Rosenzweig

Joan G. Roland, 1989
Jews in British India: Identity in a Colonial Era

Yisrael Gutman, Ezra Mendelsohn, Jehuda Reinharz, and Chone Shmeruk, editors, 1989
The Jews of Poland Between Two World Wars

Avraham Barkai, 1989
From Boycott to Annihilation: The Economic Struggle of German Jews, 1933–1943

Alexander Altmann, 1991
The Meaning of Jewish Existence: Theological Essays 1930–1939

Magdalena Opalski and Israel Bartal, 1992
Poles and Jews: A Failed Brotherhood

Richard Breitman, 1992
The Architect of Genocide: Himmler and the Final Solution

George L. Mosse, 1993
Confronting the Nation: Jewish and Western Nationalism

Daniel Carpi, 1994
Between Mussolini and Hitler: The Jews and the Italian Authorities in France and Tunisia

Walter Laqueur and Richard Breitman, 1994
Breaking the Silence: The German Who Exposed the Final Solution

Ismar Schorsch, 1994
From Text to Context: The Turn to History in Modern Judaism

Jacob Katz, 1995
With My Own Eyes: The Autobiography of an Historian

Gideon Shimoni, 1995
The Zionist Ideology

Moshe Prywes and Haim Chertok, 1996
Prisoner of Hope

János Nyiri, 1997
Battlefields and Playgrounds

Alan Mintz, editor, 1997
The Boom in Contemporary Israeli Fiction

Samuel Bak, paintings
Lawrence L. Langer, essay and commentary, 1997
Landscapes of Jewish Experience

Jeffrey Shandler and Beth S. Wenger, editors, 1997
Encounters with the "Holy Land": Place, Past and Future in American Jewish Culture

Simon Rawidowicz, 1998
State of Israel, Diaspora, and Jewish Continuity: Essays on the "Ever-Dying People"

Jacob Katz, 1998
A House Divided: Orthodoxy and Schism in Nineteenth-Century Central European Jewry

Elisheva Carlebach, John M. Efron, and David M. Myers, editors, 1998
Jewish History and Jewish Memory: Essays in Honor of Yosef Hayim Yerushalmi

Shmuel Almog, Jehuda Reinharz, and Anita Shapira, editors, 1998
Zionism and Religion

Ben Halpern and Jehuda Reinharz, 2000
Zionism and the Creation of a New Society

Walter Laqueur, 2001
Generation Exodus: The Fate of Young Jewish Refugees from Nazi Germany

Yigal Schwartz, 2001
Aharon Appelfeld: From Individual Lament to Tribal Eternity

Renée Poznanski, 2001
Jews in France during World War II

Jehuda Reinharz, 2001
Chaim Weizmann: The Making of a Zionist Leader

Jehuda Reinharz, 2001
Chaim Weizmann: The Making of a Statesman

ChaeRan Y. Freeze, 2002
Jewish Marriage and Divorce in Imperial Russia

Mark A. Raider and Miriam B. Raider-Roth, 2002
The Plough Woman: Records of the Pioneer Women of Palestine

Ezra Mendelsohn, 2002
Painting a People: Maurycy Gottlieb and Jewish Art

Alan Mintz, 2002
Reading Hebrew Literature: Critical Discussions of Six Modern Texts

Haim Be'er, 2002
The Pure Element of Time

Yehudit Hendel, 2002
Small Change: A Collection of Stories

CONTENTS

· ·

Beauty has no other source but the wound. —*Jean Genet*

ehudit Hendel is the most prominent woman in the first generation of Israeli prose writers, which includes such figures as Aharon Megged, Moshe Shamir, Natan Shaham, and Hanokh Bartov. Her writing career spans the entire history of Israel from its formative years through the last decade of the twentieth century. Born in Poland, she came to Israel as a child. Her first stories were published in the collection *They Are Different People* (1950). Her first novel, *Street of Steps* (1954), won a literary prize and was staged by the Habimah National Theater. Thanks to these early works, Hendel was the first woman author to win acclaim since Dvora Baron, the founding mother of Hebrew women's literature. Nonetheless, it was fifteen years before she published her second novel *The Yard of Momo the Great* (1969). This modernistic work was ahead of its time and was reissued in 1993 in a revised version titled *The Last Hamsin*.

In contrast to most of her literary contemporaries, Hendel did not accord the *sabra*, the native-born Israeli, the central role in her work. In stark opposition to the heroic masculine type incarnated in the *sabra*, Hendel wrote instead about people living on the margins of society. It may well be true that her intense sensitivity to suffering stems from the death of her mother when Hendel was a child. Be that as it may, her fiction describes the victims of war and of the Holocaust, the displaced, the depressed, and the terminally ill. *The Other Power* (1985) focused on the life, work, and death of her husband, the painter Zvi Mairovich, and on the madness of art. *Near Quiet Places* (1987) is a powerful collection based on her travel to Poland and the concentration camps. *The Mountain of Losses* (1991), which strongly evokes the terible suffering of bereaved parents and wives, is one of the most important works of anti-war literature in Israel.

Since the mid-1980s, Hendel's work has manifested strong feminist elements. The stories in *Small Change* (1988), like those in *An Innocent*

Breakfast (1996), depict the intimate experiences of women and protest, with stunning force, against male violence, both physical and emotional. The female characters in *Small Change* refuse victimization. The eponymous hero of "My Friend B's Feast," suffering from a terminal illness, protests, at a macabre dinner party, against her imminent replacement by another woman, thereby exposing her to all present. The heroine of the story "Small Change" uses her menstrual blood to scrawl biblical verses on the walls of a Swiss jail where she has been wrongly imprisoned: "For I am left naked and bare and for these things I weep." The insertion of these sacred verses among the obscene drawings executed by male prisoners, and her use of menstrual blood as ink, are powerful symbols of feminist protest.

Because her mission is to expose, relentlessly and without sentimentality, the travails of human existence, Hendel refuses to depict reality in logical, linear ways. The stories in *Small Change* attest to pain and loss so profound that they cannot be conveyed in more traditionally organized narratives. Instead, her "documentary" style, characterized by an uncanny grasp of the minute details of everyday living and of intense but ephemeral moments, sunders time and space, capturing the chaotic and enigmatic nature of reality. Because these stories open and close quietly, they give the impression of ragged margins; as in real life, there is no closure, only a sense of the tale as a snippet in a much wider panorama. Readers lose themselves in the text, just as the narrator has; together, they confront unprocessed pain and emotion.

The intimacy Hendel creates between reader and narrator, and between narrator and other characters, enhanced by the relaxed, almost conversational tone of these stories, is another aspect of women's writing. In the stories in *Small Change,* the narrator's ability to overcome her separateness from those around her exemplifies the feminist notion that women's sense of personal autonomy is less rigidly demarcated than men's. Accustomed to viewing themselves in relation to others, women are more immediately capable than men of empathy with others. Hendel takes this notion one step farther: in her stories, strong identification—to the point where lines differentiating people are blurred—is one of Yehudit Hendel's trademarks. The identification that allows her narrator to overcome human separateness is based on the fact that women excel at establishing self-boundaries that are more flexable than those of men. That is, women can, and tend to, include people who are close to them within their own personal identities. Diffuse boundaries are what make women more capable than men of identifying with others naturally and deeply. In "A Story with No Address," for example, the narrator identifies with a woman she is not acquainted with at all, not even by name. Yet because she is witness to the woman's collapse, she visits the hospital where the woman was taken. The narrator identifies not only with the woman but also with her dog, whose world came to an end when its owner died.

Indeed, the power and authenticity of Hendel's fiction lie in her ability to stress the pathetic precisely through the banal (the rudeness of the shopgirl, the disinterest of the doctor), and to transform an everyday expression lacking in resonance like "small change" into a richly expressive sysmbol. Characteristic of her work is her choice of a popular expression like "small change" rather than a more literary phrase. "Small change" is an expression commonly used by Israeli bus drivers. But in the story "Small Change," the bus driver's obsessive preoccupation with collecting coins symbolizes the quiet violence with which he has turned the lives of his wife and daughter into cheap currency, namely "small change."

Another trademark of women's literature is a blurred line between fantasy and reality, or art and life. While Hendel is, of course, neither the first nor the only author to make minor adaptations in genuine biographical material for use in her fiction, her efforts are especially textured. Hendel's creation of "Low, Close to the Floor," is a case in point. In the story, the narrator obtains from her father a photograph of her late mother, after he had married a second time. For years it remained as it was given, wrapped and bound. After the father dies, the narrator finally opens the package and nails the photograph low, close to the floor. The short story, crafted almost entirely as a conversation between father and daughter, centers around the father as an old man, after the death of his second wife, speaking to his daughter about the difficult choice he faces—next to which wife should he be buried? In subsequent interviews, Hendel stressed that she never thought herself capable of writing about such a traumatic personal experience. Yet, immediately after pounding the nail into the hard concrete wall, she felt an intense need to write the story. She felt she was both the nail and the one hammering it in.

Clearly, Hendel does not rely on the assorted distancing techniques used by most authors to distinguish fact from fiction. Instead, she herself becomes one with her narrators, people whose identies are themselves shaped by other characters. The intimacy established, then, between the narrator and other characters draws on, and is enriched by, the deliberately compromised identity/voice of the author. This is how Hendel connects herself, her narrators, her characters, and her readers, bringing all into a shared community of grief and salvation. Hendel seems to know the reader's pain in the same way she knows the pain of her characters. Her willingness to expose herself in this way stems from a sense that people share deep communal relationships that make all pretense unneccesary.

In the end, what makes *Small Change* women's writing is Hendel's fundamental view of reality, which can be summarized as a sense of continuous flow among people, making them inseparable. It is expressed in the extraordinary way her narrator identifies with her characters, as well as in her willingness to make use of highly personal material, even at the price of suffering—her own, and that of her characters. Such fictionalized testimony elevates real-life trauma and provides the sufferer a communal space—created by the shared experiences of the author, narrator, characters, and readers—in which to grieve and to stop grieving. One of the protagonists of *Small Change* mentions the marvelous music that Bach composed to the words "Ah world, I must leave you," music that, metaphorically speaking, echoes the goal of Hendel's fiction: to redeem harsh reality through the denser, richer medium of art.

Translated by Natalie Mendelsohn and Chaya Galai

SMALL CHANGE

n Friday, when I went to the store on the corner to buy a newspaper, a tall woman in a white dress was standing there smoking. Next to her was a little dog and I saw her lean over to the dog and then there was a hoarse shriek: You crazy, putting out cigarettes on the floor? That's how you smoke?

The woman straightened up slowly and adjusted the white collar of her dress.

I'm sorry, she said.

Sorry, the shriek again; sorry? You put cigarettes out on the floor? A pasty saliva foam bubbled on the girl's lips and she stuck out her tongue and licked it off.

I'm sorry, said the woman.

The coarse voice kept on.

Some nerve you got to say you're sorry, it shrieked, burn my foot and say you're sorry, stand in a store with a great big dog and burn my foot and say you're sorry, that's how you smoke, lady?

The woman, very pale, didn't budge.

I'm sorry, she said.

The girl stamped. She went on in a hoarse voice, arms flailing, eyes blazing back and forth, as if she had two heads, the one in front and the one in back.

You're crazy, you say you're sorry, you burn my foot and say you're sorry, you don't see you burned my foot, you don't see I'm barefoot?

The dog stood up on his hind legs and clambered up the woman.

I'm sorry, I'm really sorry, she said. She was growing paler. I didn't see you were barefoot.

The girl kept stamping both feet. They were bare and particularly big, the toes splayed like asymmetrical stems growing out of the floor. A narrow pasty strip fizzed on her face.

You didn't see? she screamed. Puts out cigarettes on my foot and says she didn't see. Where'd you grow up, lady?

Quiet, said the newspaper man.

What quiet? screamed the girl. She licked her chin, which was also covered with the damp white pasty foam. What quiet? she screamed.

The dog shrank back from the woman's legs. All of a sudden he whined.

Can I have a chair? said the woman.

Burns up my foot and wants a chair, shouted the girl. These dames have some nerve—

The dog was whining faster, drier.

Can I have a chair? whispered the woman. Her face took on the shade of a paper bag. Do you have a telephone? she whispered.

The newspaper man didn't hear.

Maybe you have a telephone, she whispered.

The dog jumped on her, clasped her in the heat of his despair with his mouth and paws. He twisted around, riveted himself into a circle, backed off and stood up on his hind legs, his thin ankles rigid.

The woman sighed a soft sigh of pain. She tottered back a bit and forward a bit, her head leaning on her shoulder. Then she dropped onto the chair, with a thump, as if she were falling onto the floor.

I think you should call an ambulance, somebody said.

Ambulance? screamed the girl. Burns my foot and needs an ambulance. They get away with murder, she shouted.

The dog stood erect on his hind legs. A strange noise was coming from his belly.

By the time the ambulance came, the woman was barely breathing. The doctors refused to take the dog in the ambulance. He twisted around again, riveted himself into a circle, hanging on the back door that was still wide open. Then I saw him running among the cars, like a wild animal, whining all the while.

In the evening I went to Ikhilov Hospital. That night it wasn't the hospital on call for emergencies so the yard was almost empty. The dog lay outside, scratching himself. When he saw me he turned his head and stared at me. His eyes were red as two red cherries.

In the hospital admissions offices, no one knew anything. I said that a woman with a dog was brought in at noon.

No dog, said the clerk.

I said he was still outside, the dog.

What dog? said the clerk.

The doctor sitting at the desk twitched his shoulders.

Oh, the one from the newspaper store, he said. He looked very tired. He said there was no address. They looked in her purse. No address. He asked if I would like to identify the body.

I said I didn't know the woman.

Too bad, he said, somebody has to identify the body.

I asked when she died.

Oh, he said, she was dead on arrival. He looked at me for a moment, steadily, blankly. There wasn't any dog. He looked at me again with the same blank, glassy-eyed stare. You can get her clothes in the morgue, he said.

I said she was wearing a white dress.

Could be, he said, I didn't see a white dress.

Yes, she was buying newspapers, I said, she was wearing a white dress.

Maybe, said the doctor, there weren't any newspapers. He raised his head and looked at me again. He said he hadn't seen any white dress. A vague smile hovered over his face.

He asked if it made a difference that she was wearing a white dress. Anyway, somebody has to identify the body, he said.

The clerk said there was a dog.

Now the doctor stared at the clerk. He said he didn't know if they'd take a dog's identification.

In fact, why not? said the clerk.

Yes, said the doctor, but anyway, the dog won't be able to take care of the funeral arrangements.

The dog leaped up wildly as if he had been shot. He jumped on the doctor.

Oh no, said the doctor.

The dog didn't let go. Afterward he walked silently behind the doctor and I didn't see him go into the morgue. I only saw him come out. He walked slowly, rubbing his back on the wall. Instead of saliva, drops of blood came from his throat. Then he stuck himself to the chair in the corridor, his back twisted, as if he were glued to the chair. He scratched both eyes with one of his legs and uttered a strange sound, like someone sawing through a board.

I returned home along King David Boulevard. By now it was dusk. The boulevard was empty. The trees were tall thin pale noisy and quiet.

Next to me walked a guy with a Walkman clamped to his ears. Behind me, mute and patient, walked the dog. His small body was big and he walked along dead, his jaw stiff as a hoof. The guy with the Walkman came very close to me. He was wearing a bright red t-shirt that glowed like a traffic light on the boulevard. He took the earphones off for a moment. He said: A million men built the Great Wall of China. I didn't catch what he said. He smiled and turned around to me. A million men built the Great Wall of China, he repeated and again took off the earphones. He asked if I wanted to hear. I said there was a dog walking behind me. He looked at me very closely and said there wasn't any dog here. I said I clearly saw him walking. Then the guy with the Walkman smiled again. A million men built the Great Wall of China, he said, and that's the only thing they see from outer space, you understand? He put his earphones back on and turned the knob, which emitted a wild music. You understand? he repeated. The music came from him as if it were coming out of his body, like a long chromatic wail. He made a half turn to me. Whales love the saxophone, he said, I don't know what dogs love. He lowered his voice and smiled a bit too broadly. Maybe the saxophone, too, he said. In the dusk, the pupils of his eyes looked very bright. I love the saxophone, too, he said, don't you? There wasn't anybody on the boulevard except me, the guy with the Walkman and the dog who went on walking dead, his jaw stiff, walking like stray dogs who walk around on the roads for years. The guy with the Walkman took another step. He walked slowly, absorbed in his wild music, long and shut tight like a suitcase.

It was a solemn night. The boulevard was still empty and the streets were empty too. The guy with the Walkman took another step and then was swallowed up in the boulevard, his red t-shirt glowing. He lifted his head from time to time. He looked as if he were bobbing up and down in the sea.

I thought it was time to go home. But the dog kept walking behind me dead and I said to myself, because he was dead he would walk behind me forever. His face was sad and thin and the leaves wrote a tattooed inscription on his back. Once again I saw him leap onto the woman in the white dress, caress her in the heat of his despair with his mouth and his paws. Suddenly I recalled that the Egyptians would touch the eyes and mouth of the dead to restore the senses and that's just what the dog had done. Wrapped in sawdust and rags, the dead gradually dried out there. When it dried, the mummy was adorned with a mask and the coffin was borne on a wooden litter shaped like a boat to eternity. Then they embalmed the soul of the dead and made a sarcophagus for the soul.

When I entered the house the television was on. They were announcing a plague of locusts in South Africa and a release of prisoners in the Philippines. The announcer said it was a yellowish-white locust and millions of the pests were spreading over forests and fields, destroying every strip of green and they showed Jeeps riding and spraying poison and black workers celebating because, for them, the locust was a delicacy. Then they showed the funeral of a youth blown up by a mine in Lebanon. The mother was waving her hands and shouting. The rabbi was nodding his head. Saying Holy Holy. It was hot and he was sweating a lot. The mother was ripping her arms off her body. The rabbi kept nodding his head. Saying Holy Holy. The mother was kneeling on the earth. Then they showed the dignitaries who attended the funeral. They were wearing big sunglasses and were sweating under their sunglasses and wiping away their sweat. The rabbi began the *El Male Rakhamin*. The mother was eating the earth.

I turned off the television and made some coffee. I thought about the woman in the white dress. Then I thought about the dog and I wondered if anyone came to identify the body. All of a sudden I remembered Paul Celan and that his body floated on the Seine. The Paris gendarmes no doubt cursed when they found his body floating on the Seine. I didn't know if he had papers on him and if they had to identify the body, I didn't know what bridge, I didn't know if it was day or night, summer or winter, and it seemed to me that he floated in a black suit. I called my friend in Haifa. She said: What? What suit? Oh, no, he didn't think about that. He closed himself up in a room and didn't come out. It was in a school. He taught in a school. He couldn't. Couldn't what, I asked. Live, she said. I asked if it was summer or winter. She didn't remember. And the bridge? I asked. She was silent. No, she didn't know if there was a bridge. No, she didn't know where it was. Again she was silent. The Seine is so slow, she said. Now I remembered when we were in Venice we went to the island where Saint Francis had talked to the birds. They were selling jars of colored Venetian glass there. The glass was beautiful but the jars were ugly and I asked: Where are the birds? And Zvi said: You see, they sell eyes of crystal and you can buy yellow eyes here you can buy red eyes you can buy horse's eyes, cats have green pupils, he said, and here they're selling a green pupil, it's the iron-oxidation that makes them green that makes them see at night, that's because the glass is strong under pressure that's why it's so fragile, lets the light through so much, ninety percent of the light so many years so many generations, come, he said, there must be the birds. My friend in Haifa asked why I broke off the conversation. I said I hadn't broken off the conversation.

The next day I went back to the hospital. There wasn't any dog there and I returned along the boulevard. There wasn't any dog there either, neither living nor dead nor walking along the boulevard. I remembered my mother once told me there is no need to be afraid of the dead. That was back in Nesher, when we lived near the cemetery, when I was a little girl. How old was I then? How old am I now? How old was she? How old is she now? There's nothing to fear from the gravestones, she said, they're made of stone. You think there's no life in stone? I said to my mother. The wind changes the shape of the stone, I said to my mother. Oh no, said my mother, only time.

She used to comb her hair in front of a small mirror on a white lacquered board. I was a girl when they brought her personal belongings. What happened to them to those personal belongings of hers? She didn't die, said my father's father. She just went away. My father didn't answer. And my father's father left. Then he came back. His coat was wet and his face was wet too and he didn't go to my father, he just wiped his face with his coat and said: First day last day they blow the shofar and shout and pray, and my father didn't answer.

It was early in the morning when she went away. She was forty years old when she went away. I didn't know then how young she was. They use the cypress to make musical instruments, she told me once. That was when the cypress near our shack died. Maybe it will be a musical instrument, she told me once. Dry wood is strong, she said.

I was alone with her that early morning. The balcony was filled with light. The garden was filled with light. She sighed one weak sigh. I went out to the balcony and stood there. Even today I remember the light.

How old was she then? How old is she now? What did I know then? What do I know now? You think you learn that, she told me once. Look at the windows when they're closed, she said. Those black holes absorbing distress, oh no, this she didn't say.

. . .

I went home quickly. I quickly made myself some coffee and quickly turned on the radio. Someone on the radio was saying that in Portugal they decorated the city with tens of thousands of paper flowers, the whole city was paper flowers, all the houses and all the people and even the electrical poles. I changed the station. Someone was talking about spots on the sun. The sunwind is emitted from the areas of sunspots, he said, and the convergence of a few sunspots absorbs enormous amounts of radiation. His voice was soft and I stayed on the station. He spoke slowly and I listened to his soft, musical voice. How the sun emits a sunwind like a sprinkler and something about the space surrounding the sun and how the sunwind there is strong and great.

Why do sunspots appear in various areas, he asked, why is it a cycle of eleven years. The activity of the sun isn't guaranteed either. Will changes take place in the sun, in the sunwind, he asked. I pressed my ear to the radio. He said there was a period of seventy years without sunspots.

Without sunspots? I said into the radio. The corona of the sun disappeared, he said from the radio. I turned off the radio.

The next day I went back to the hospital. The doctor wasn't there this time either. The clerk said she didn't know anything. Every day there are dead people here, she said.

I asked if they had buried the dog, too.

She said you have to ask about dead dogs at city hall.

I returned along the boulevard. The boulevard was empty now too and I sat down on a bench. It was hot. The trees were tall and sharpened like tips of white thorns and a narrow white path was hanging over the trees.

Translated by Barbara Harshav

Everyone said she was just wonderful, that she behaved perfectly during the funeral. She didn't cry, and wasn't stony, either. She was just quiet. Under the black hat she was very pale, now even more than usual, since she was pale before anyhow. She shook hands and said thank you and even looked people in the eye, her fierce blue eyes, and she did it naturally, she wasn't making an effort. At the entrance to the cemetery she was already asking the people to come home with her, that, too, very quietly. "Come on up for a while," she said. The house was clean, even tidy. You'd never have thought that yesterday they took her husband out of there dead. There was even food, and it looked as if, early in the morning, before the funeral, she'd gone shopping and set it all up. Even the two daughters—Michelle's daughters, his first wife—were surprised. They said they hadn't prepared anything, she'd done everything herself. First of all, they'd been so shocked, and besides, the babies, they both had babies. In fact, they were the ones who walked around nervous, disappearing every once in a while, making everyone tense and uncomfortable, while she went on serving, quietly, asking each of the guests if they wanted tea or coffee, black or with milk, and oh my, I forgot you like lots of milk, I'm so sorry, she said, and take some cookies, they're very good, really.

And people really did feel good, especially the closest ones, who had been a little worried. There were also the neighbors, of course. Come in, come in, she said. The truth is, it was us, Rina and I, who came in first, and even then everything was ready for an ordinary visit. The pillows were all arranged on the sofa, and the chairs as usual stood around the sofa, and then the two armchairs. On the buffet there were baked things spread out, tender and flaky, the way she was always saying, flaky, and in the kitchen the teacups with the little handles were ready, and mugs for coffee, and big plates and small plates and bowls, and of course here and there on the buffet were Emmanuel's stones, his fossils, since Emmanuel used to collect fossils and had horse fossils and fish fossils and ring fossils and eye fossils, and there were fingers and swords, and there were some where it was hard to tell whether they were fingers or swords. As usual, among the fossils stood the cookies, and there were a few different kinds of cookies and a few kinds of crackers, and there were dates and figs and of course almonds and raisins and walnuts, but those maybe she had in the house beforehand because Emmanuel liked dried fruit, and whenever we went there we used to crack some nuts and munch a few peanuts with dried fruit, which is what we were doing that day, too, as I said, and everything very relaxed. At first it rained. Then it cleared up. She asked if it was stuffy in there and opened the window. They said it wasn't stuffy but she could open the window, and fresh air poured into the room, fresh air from the trees and from the mountain. She said Emmanuel liked the windows open even in the wind, he liked the air coming with wind from the mountain, and she said it so quietly that it wasn't embarrassing, it was even nice, and one of the people there said: Yes, this week I saw him walking on the boulevard. Yes, said Mikela, at night we would go out for a little walk. One of the neighbors, the one with the curls, said yes in fact she had seen them walking in the park, and it was nice, and the other neighbor said: Whenever people saw you it was nice. She said it in a loud voice, warmly, and the atmosphere later too was relaxed. The conversation flowed. One of the neighbors said that he was really a lucky person, because even for dying a person needs luck, and he died at home, everyone knows how much nicer it is to die at home, and the other neighbor confirmed. She said it was really nice to die at home, everyone would wish himself that, to die at home, and in such a pleasant home, she said. After that, as usual, someone asked how it happened. Mikela was in the middle of pouring the coffee then and she continued to pour carefully, bending over the hot coffee pot. She said: Simply, he died. He said something and died. Someone asked what. She said: Nothing, just nothing. The two twins who were sitting on the stools shifted to get up. They asked what. Really, nothing, just nothing, she said. That's what I want to know, said the big twin. Mikela didn't answer. The steam from the coffee pot was climbing up her face and she wiped it with a flick of the hand.

The last word my father said. The big twin pulled herself up.

Mikela didn't answer. She was still holding the pot of coffee with her two hands, quiet the whole time.

I didn't hear it, she said.

I think it is my right to know the last word my father said, the big twin repeated.

Mikela moved the coffee pot away from her body. Now she was holding it in the air with two hands, a little strangely, at a distance from her body, looking neither right nor left.

The last word that came out of his mouth when he was alive, said the big twin.

Mikela was still standing with the pot in the same strange position, looking neither right nor left.

He was already dead, she said.

And you kept him to yourself dead all night, said the big twin.

There was silence.

You only called in the morning.

There was silence. The coffee pot must have really been hot, because she passed it like that, standing up, through the air, far away from her stomach, from one hand to the other, without shifting her eyes, looking ahead in the same strange way, quiet the whole time. Then she went over to the buffet and set it down, bending, wiping the drops of moisture from her face, returning to the center of the room, and there suddenly stopped, crossing one leg over the other and standing in the middle of the room, on one leg, like a stork. I didn't want to wake you, she said, standing like that on one leg, in the middle of the room, like a stork, keeping her silence and calm all the time, and that's the silence I remembered afterwards, when everyone asked when she had decided what she decided, and the private little deal she made with Fate, the silence that, it seemed, she would forget when she awakened from it, continuing in that slow, indifferent way of talking, and then someone said, like Isadora Duncan, naked under her scarves. But she didn't answer. She smiled under her scarves, now without the black hat that brought out her pallor, holding an unlighted cigarette between her lips and asking for a light, oh, I forgot my lighter, I've lost my lighter, maybe somebody has seen my lighter, she said.

We were talking about my father's last word, said the big twin.

There was no last word, she said.

His last word when he was alive, said the big twin.

Mikela didn't answer. She said something like it'll pass, something I didn't catch, her hands grasping her elbows, taking shallow breaths like somebody sleeping, looking straight ahead in no direction, into the air, with eyes almost unmoving, focused in a narrow space straight ahead, and her face got paler and paler, more and more the color of a pearl, so shiny that I thought was it white pearl or black pearl and how fast, too fast, everything happened, short, too short in this strange tranquillity, as the little twin sobbed. And that too I remembered afterwards, the "it'll pass," the emptiness in her voice, still standing the way she was, not connected to anything, on one leg, and it seemed to me that it wasn't her saying it, only her voice, which had a tinny sound, rhythmic, like a gutter hit by rain.

She coughed.

I'm sorry I'm hoarse, she said and turned around to smile.

I've lost my voice, she said, and again turned around to smile. There was an odd clarity in her icy eyes. She went over to the buffet, took a bowl of dried fruit and passed among the chairs. Please, please, she said, bending over and serving.

It was a small apartment, two rooms, and the door to the bedroom was closed, so everyone sat crowded together in the one room, on armchairs and chairs and stools they brought in from the kitchen, and on the sofa. There were people that I knew and people I didn't know. On my right was the neighbor with the curly hair, and on the other side a man who was smoking a pipe in the light armchair. He tamped the tobacco down in his pipe, talking with the man in the rocking chair. In Chile alone there are two thousand volcanoes, he said to the man in the rocking chair, and leaned forward a bit with his pipe. The man in the rocking chair laughed. The last generation of volcanoes, he said. Just then Mikela was offering the bowl of candied orange rind to the man in the armchair. Please, please, she said. The top half of her body leaned forward. It's excellent, really, she said, bringing the bowl closer to him. I'm sure it is, said the man with the pipe, putting his pipe down on the arm of the chair and taking a handful of the candied fruit. He chewed it slowly, looking at Mikela, who was now bent over the man in the rocking chair. It's excellent, she was saying now too. The man in the rocking chair leaned over and took one candied strip, gnawing at the sugar, which made a little squeak. He licked his lips, which also made a little sugar squeak. Sorry, he said, still nibbling at the candied rind, his eyes focused on her face, and suddenly there was a panicked-bird look on her face. She straightened up and with the palm of her hand brushed back a bunch of hair that had fallen into her face, with a heavy movement as if her hair hurt. Then she smoothed it over her ears and pressed.

Really, it's excellent, she said again.

Uncle Eliahu drew up his knees. Slowly he lifted his head toward her, with a pained smile.

In the summer, when I went with Emmanuel to Poland, we went to their town and found the house. Poles were living in the house. They had a clock with little legs, that stood there on the credenza, and when they left, they had left it on the credenza. It still showed the same time.

The same time? said the little twin.

The same time, said Uncle Eliahu. He sighed, giving Mikela a pained smile. You know the story, don't you, Mikela?

The big twin turned sharply in her chair. You know the story? she said.

Mikela again smoothed the hair over her ears, pressing hard.

Yes, she said, since then the clock has stood still. Only a week ago he was telling me that.

Daddy never told me that, said the little twin, he told you that?

Yes, said Mikela, he told me that many times. The new tenants never wound the clock, he said.

The little twin said that was a terrible story.

Daddy used to love to tell it, said Mikela.

He used to tell you stories? said the little twin.

He quoted Bach, he said that Bach wrote music for the line: Oh world, I have to leave you now. He wrote wonderful music for that, choral music.

Choral music? said the little twin.

Yes, for men's choruses and women's choruses and boys' choruses. He used to set them up, dressed in black and white, on a black-and-white tile floor, like chess.

There was silence. She smiled, close-mouthed, the bowl of candied rinds in her hand, then took a thin strip of gold rind, brought it up to her face, and put it back.

There's an ancient Indian saying: The music goes on, only we fade away, she said, holding the candied rind in her hand and putting it back in the bowl. It's coming down harder, she said, and put the bowl down on the buffet. Her voice was low, without changing pace, as if the tones went backwards, from the end to the beginning.

There was silence. You could hear rain pounding harder. It flooded the garden with real force. It's coming down harder, she said again, and went to the window. On the other side of the glass was the vigorous motion of trunks and treetops, and she pressed her face against the pane, opened it a crack and took a deep breath. Thick, cold air seeped into the room, and the odor of damp earth, a sourish smell of vegetation and soil. She put her face out the window, breathing deeply, and held it outside, her face in the frame of the window. It looked white, thin, distorted through the glass, crushed in the wind, barely able to stand the pressure on her body. She closed the window, passing her hand over the area of distortion, over the neck and the nape, and you could read in her face that weight in the nape, yearning for someone to shout, for her to shout, but of course no shout was heard. She wiped the spray from her face, and again took a deep breath. Her gaze dimmed.

You're tired, said Aunt Eva.

Mikela didn't answer. She was still standing, heavy, drawn down, her body breaking of its own heat. She hunched her shoulders a bit, with small shrugging movements, the way you do when your bones feel cold.

I'll make you some tea, said Aunt Eva. You must sit down.

Mikela straightened up in panic. She stretched her neck out, holding it high, as if nailing her head on.

No need, she said.

But we can see you're tired, Aunt Eva repeated.

Oh no, said Mikela, alarmed. Her face changed all at once. I have guests.

Uncle Eliahu, leaning over the table at the other side of the room, kept on: My brother went with us then. He went with a black beard and came back with white. Eliahu made little fluttery motions with his hands as if trying to put the different pictures together.

Went there with black and came back with white, he said.

That was before, said the big twin.

Uncle Eliahu evidently didn't hear.

Then, when you went to Poland that was before, she repeated.

Stop it, stop it, sobbed the little twin.

But it was before, the big twin repeated.

Stop it, sobbed the little twin.

Uncle Eliahu squirmed in his chair. It's terrible, he said. He murmured something, licking his lips as if he felt dry in the mouth.

I'll put up coffee, said Mikela.

Did you say something? said the little twin, still sobbing.

I'll put up coffee, said Mikela. She said that in any case she'd have to put up a new pot, in any case the other was finished. The little twin, who apparently hadn't been listening, got caught on the word "finished." She swallowed saliva, choking back her sobs.

What? she said.

The two people in the armchairs moved closer to each other, rolling their chairs on small coasters, deep in conversation. In order for petroleum to be formed, there has to be a dense mass of rock with animals caught beneath it, in instant burial, said the man in the armchair. That's it, said the man in the chair, as far as "hot spots" and minerals. What? said the little twin. The man in the armchair turned his head. No, we're talking, he said. The little twin suddenly faced the man in the armchair. He really did love to tell stories, she said.

Nice, said the man in the armchair.

The little twin gazed at him, livening up. Yes, when I was a little girl he always loved to tell stories.

Nice, the man in the armchair repeated.

The little twin paused a moment, her eyes burning into Mikela. He used to tell about the mountain that goes all around the world, she said. When she was a little girl he always used to tell about that. He said there were stones that lit up at night, and once she asked him where, and he said: There, on the mountain that goes all around the world. He didn't tell you that? she asked.

Mikela shook herself, straightened up, and went on serving dried fruit in silence, walking around like a huge rind of herself.

You didn't answer me, said the little twin.

Mikela remained standing for a moment, passing the empty pot from one hand to the other.

In New York the clocks say: the time is twelve-o-five and six seconds. They think that clock-time matters, she said.

And you? said the big twin.

Mikela didn't budge.

And you? The big twin wouldn't let up. You think clock-time matters?

Mikela didn't budge. The pot shook a little in her hands.

Here, what time is it now, for instance. Five-o-six. Yesterday at this time it was also five-o-six.

Yes, said the man in the armchair.

The man in the chair said there are many kinds of time.

Yes, said the man in the armchair.

The man in the chair said there are many kinds of time.

Yes, there are some people who are always late, she said.

And those who aren't late? said the man in the chair.

Their times are exact, they don't burn up in passages.

The big twin asked what does that mean, in passages?

Mikela was still standing with the coffee pot. She raised her eyes and I saw her walleyed gaze, the eyes fleeing each other, as if they'd forgotten which way to move. She said: That's an expression of Daddy's, Daddy used to say that.

Yes, said the man in the armchair, you forgot that your dad was an expert in geological layers.

At the time I still didn't know who the man in the armchair was, and only afterwards did I understand that he was a geologist too, and that he was head of the department, which is what Emmanuel was supposed to become next year, but unlike Emmanuel he dealt with the major rifts and not geological layers.

Mikela didn't seem to be listening.

It's coming down harder, she said again, turning toward the kitchen, but still standing there, the coffee pot in her hands. She asked what time it was. No, I'm not tired, she said, and asked the time again. Her blue eyes were as grey as glass then. Really, I'm not tired, she said.

You didn't sleep, said Aunt Eva.

Oh, no, I have guests, she said.

Uncle Eliahu whispered something to Aunt Eva, who started to get up, but at the same moment in walked a tall girl, filling the whole doorway, calling out: Hi, how's it going? The man in the chair said: Okay, nothing new. And you? Great, she said, and you? The man in the chair said: The usual, nothing new. What's in the paper? The tall girl, who was holding a newspaper, said that again a girl had been raped in North Tel Aviv and in Bat Yam an old woman was murdered. They broke into her apartment and tied something around her neck and strangled her neck. She had a gold chain on her neck. The man in the armchair chuckled into his pipe. He said a gold chain is a wondrous thing, with gold souls can be ushered into heaven. The tall girl laughed loudly. Oh no, she said, into earth. The man in the armchair, who was not listening, said again that Emmanuel really was an expert in geological layers. The little twin bent over, staring at her feet. After that she fixed her gaze on the man in the armchair.

An interesting profession, said the tall girl.

Mikela was just coming out of the kitchen, after putting more water up to boil, and she stopped, the upper part of her body tilting slightly backward, as if she was leaning on some invisible railing, again quiet the whole time. She was looking at the man in the armchair.

He loved the apple model, she said. There was deep longing in her voice.

Someone asked what's the apple model.

The cooling apple, she said. She was speaking slowly, holding back the fear you could sense from the longing in her voice.

Ah well, said the man in the armchair, there's this theory, pretty well known, that mountains are the earth's wrinkles.

Mountain ranges, the man in the rocking chair corrected.

What? said Uncle Eliahu.

Mountain ranges, he repeated, like in an apple when it's baking.

What? Uncle Eliahu asked again.

The man in the armchair adjusted his position. He said that the earth is like an apple, that is a baked apple, when you take it out of the oven it shrinks and gets wrinkles in its skin, and that's how it is with the earth, that is, with the earth's crust, it shrinks and gets wrinkles in its skin, and those wrinkles are the mountains, he said.

Uncle Eliahu, at the end of the table, pressed his hands hard against his chest.

The mountains? he said.

Actually, the mountain ranges, the man in the armchair corrected.

Odd, said Uncle Eliahu.

The man in the armchair surveyed the company. He noted that meanwhile things had changed, meanwhile people had begun to think differently, but Emmanuel was very busy with the formation of mountains.

Interesting, said the tall girl again. She laughed out loud: What interesting things there are.

The man in the armchair surveyed the company again, smiling with pleasure. He said that study of the oceans, for instance, had revealed amazing things, like wrinkled layers of sedimentary rock. He paused a moment, surveying his audience. It turns out that what happens in the depths of the ocean influences continental drift and the formation of mountain ranges, he said.

Interesting, said the tall girl once more. She asked how.

Ah well, it's complicated, said the man in the armchair.

Oh, come on, said the tall girl.

Very complicated, said the man in the armchair. But it's known that the formation of oceans begins on land, along the "fault line" on land.

Uncle Eliahu sighed. Like a man, he said, really starts in the earth.

The man in the armchair smiled. He took out a penknife and cleaned his pipe, then brushed the remains of tobacco from his pants, folded the knife and put it in his pocket.

No, said Uncle Eliahu, better to say he ends up in the earth. He suddenly gagged. I would like to understand what he did, he said. He asked the head of the department if he understood what Emmanuel did.

Not very well, said the department head, not very well. We understand only a little. He asked to have some tea if he could. He had smoked too much that day.

Mikela said she was sorry. She said she'd prepare a new pot. She was really slipping up. She'd forgotten that coffee was too heavy for him and that he liked tea. She should have thought of that, should have remembered, she was really slipping up, she repeated.

The department head, who was evidently not paying attention, asked what she hadn't remembered.

That coffee is too heavy for you, she said.

The department chairman smiled, satisfied. He said it was all right. He'd only been at their place twice, after all, and she didn't have to remember. Mikela insisted. She repeated that she'd really slipped up. Even then she'd given him decaffeinated coffee and not black the way she had today. She remembered exactly. It was after Emmanuel finished the work.

And you remember what coffee I drank at the time? said the department head.

She didn't answer, but glanced at him for a moment. Yes, I remember, she said, I remember that I put a lot of milk in your coffee, and I remember what you said then, I remember that you said you hate black coffee, is it true that you hate black coffee?

Ah well, said the department head. He smiled, following her hand gestures. She had long, beautiful hands, and when she spoke she spread them out in long, expansive gestures, as if motionless.

I remember that you said then that an ocean, like a man, has a lifespan, youth and old age.

And death, said the department head.

Yes, said Mikela, you said then that in the faculty you have a chart of an ocean that says "here lies."

The tall girl laughed loudly.

The man in the armchair stretched himself out. As a matter of fact, there is a theory that the oceans are the "silent and steady" part of the earth, he said, and again surveyed his audience with pleasure.

You talk like Emmanuel, said Mikela.

I'm sorry, said the man in the armchair.

Uncle Eliahu shifted nervously on his chair. You have to rest, he said.

I'm okay, said Mikela.

We can see you didn't sleep a wink all night, said Uncle Eliahu.

It's okay, said Mikela. Nothing to worry about, and anyway I have guests, she said.

She now poured the tea for the man in the armchair, with her beautiful sweeping gestures, carefully giving him, with the little tongs, little slices of lemon on the plate in the corner, asking: Two teaspoons? Seems to me you take two teaspoons. She brought the sugar bowl toward him, bending over him, from time to time twitching her head, like someone getting a haircut and feeling the scissors on her scalp. She smiled coldly. Have you ever felt your hands were turning into two boards, she had said to me not long before, have you ever seen a whale? Like a whale, she said, an island that just sinks, and its sailors with it. That was not long ago, not so long ago at all. We were walking on the beach, the two of us, in the evening. The beach was buzzing with people and cars and motorcycles and dogs. The sand was warm, and we were walking, the two of us, on the warm sand, and she said she loved to walk on the sand when it was warm, loved the warmth that came from the sand and went straight into the soles of her feet and climbed up her body through the soles of her feet, and she laughed. After that she said that once people used to walk all along the beach, and I asked what beach and she didn't answer. Don't you think it's great to walk along the beach? she said. Suddenly I saw her face by the grave, when they took the covering off the stretcher and lowered the wrapped man and she stood looking down. Then someone hammered a small stake in there, in the mound of mud that got higher and higher and on the stake it said: Emmanuel. The earth was wet. The stake went in quickly. A light rain sprinkled the name Emmanuel and a strong wind blew and the stake wobbled a bit. The handwriting danced. The name Emmanuel glistened wet. She stood there. And they said to her come on, come on, it's raining, but she stood there. The mushroom of umbrellas dispersed quickly and they said to her come on, come on, it's raining Mikela, it's raining, but she stood there. And someone went up to her and held an umbrella over her head to protect her from the lashes of the rain, and she stood there with her hand over her mouth and the little bit of earth that she had on her hand filled up her mouth.

When was it? Not this afternoon. Big white waves were crashing on the beach the whole way home, when we went together, squeezed into the little car. She didn't say a word the whole way. Quiet. Quiet. Looking. The tall palms along the road swayed back and forth in the wind, which was gathering force. Everything moved. The sea moved. The beach fled. She sat. She looked. Floating on the high white waves were drowned birds, drowned heads, wings, and boards and bathing caps. She sat. She looked. Everything rose. Everything sank. The seaweed. The dead algae. The dead dogs. The breakers. Tatters of dresses and coats on the breakers. And the drowned lights. The drowned dirges. She sat. She looked. It was three o'clock. She closed her bag.

Suddenly I remembered that at Nesher, when I was a kid, I was once given a board with dried butterflies on it and there were larvae with six eyes, six eyes on each side, dried with the eyes and stuck with pins to the board, and there were big white-winged butterflies and brown butterflies in coffee-color and earth-colors and yellow-winged night butterflies wrapped in wreaths of gold hairs, and butterflies with owl eyes, and my mother, who didn't like the board, said the butterflies had owl eyes, and there were butterflies with a death's head on their chest, the Death's-Head Glider, my mother said, and she said it flies light, it's the lightest butterfly, and its fluttering motions are big and give it more body heat when it flies, the one that flutters in the summer on the windows and walls, she said, and the death's head is drawn on its chest when it flutters, and it likes eggplants and potatoes and tobacco. That's exactly what it likes, she said.

The department head said he had to correct himself, for the sake of accuracy, and in things like this one must be accurate, he said he was sorry, but Emmanuel dealt mainly with basalt, and basalt is found on the ocean floor as well, and if we are to be accurate—he dealt mainly with the matter of magnets, that is to say a mineral made of an iron oxide called magnetite, and to be more exact, the magnetic pockets, and he was even on the verge of some important discovery in the field, and wasn't it too bad.

That sounds terrific, said the tall girl.

The department head asked what.

The magnetic pockets, said the tall girl.

The department head laughed.

Still, said the tall girl. She said she really loved things like that.

Uncle Eliahu asked what things.

Things you can't understand, said the tall girl.

The department head asked if she did understand other things.

Like what? she said.

The department head laughed. Aha, he said, that's the question, that's the question.

Uncle Eliahu sighed. He said that's life, you think you're getting somewhere, and then—

Then you die, said the tall girl, and put on an American accent: What're you gonna do, such is life.

Uncle Eliahu said he didn't like it when people talked that way, he didn't like it when an Israeli girl put on an American accent.

But that's the way it is, said the tall girl, hey, that's the way it is, isn't it? She laughed out loud for no reason. That's the way it is, such is life, isn't it? She turned partway toward the two twins and asked what month they were born in.

Both of us? said the big twin.

The tall girl laughed wildly. And you? she asked Mikela.

The big twin said: Scorpio. Mikela's a Scorpio.

Oh boy, said the tall girl. She stared at Mikela in amusement. Scorpio stings only itself to death, she said.

That's ridiculous, said the big twin.

The tall girl didn't react, her eyes eagerly gulping Mikela. She put on her sunglasses and lit a cigarette. Why ridiculous? she said. She turned to the department head, who was nodding his head, deep in conversation with the man in the rocking chair, and again laughed wildly at what he answered. The man in the armchair said that even rock—heat and pressure change its shape. Mikela was just then pouring him tea. She stood bending over him and said quietly into the tea: Yes, even the internal structure of the rock, without melting it. The man in the armchair stirred his tea slowly and looked slowly at her. The tall girl kept at it. And a fault in the earth? she said. A fault, too, the movement isn't constant, said the man in the armchair. For example? she said. For example, three centimeters a year, said the man in the armchair. He said the tea was delicious, he loved tea with no aroma, and Mikela gave him tea with no aroma. What a killer, said the tall girl. The department head asked what. The three centimeters a year, she said. The department head smiled into the tea. A great story, said the tall girl. Mikela didn't reply. She stood now too, quiet, very quiet, the skin of her face gleaming like pearls, like before, white pearls and black pearls, and it seemed to me so cold that if it touched fire it would put it out. There was no sign from her, no sign from her even now, and I looked at her even now, tall, thin, like a drainpipe, rain seeping down inside her body, and always asking the time, lifting her face a little and standing there, calm, looking at the wall, bending down again, offering cookies, saying again it's okay, asking do you prefer coffee or tea, I forgot you like coffee, I'm so sorry, and every time she said "it's okay" it seemed to me glass shattered inside her body. I remembered that once I saw a draft of a paper of his, and it said on it: Have the rocks moved away from each other? Were the rocks pushed? He had a small, rounded handwriting, and the word "rocks" looked like a little sketch. The transition from hard rock to soft rock creates cliffs and small valleys, why does a valley disappear? It said there in the handwriting of a little sketch, and after all I met Mikela through Emmanuel, because the one who was our friend was actually Emmanuel, that is, a friend of Zvi's, Zvi loved to eat breakfast with him in the cafe, sat with him for hours at breakfast, hearing him talk about the layers of the earth. Have the rocks moved away from each other, he would ask, were the rocks pushed? Even for earthquakes there are instruments of measurement, Emmanuel, only how does the blood get sick, Emmanuel, that we'll never know. The iron that turns to basalt is a weak magnet, Emmanuel, and love, what people call love, Emmanuel, what you said you weren't willing to give up, Emmanuel, and the model of the cooling apple, you remember, Emmanuel, the cooling apple, the apple that gets wrinkled after it's baked, Mikela would follow you anywhere, Emmanuel, and after all even the oceans, you used to say, are born in the earth, and the death of an ocean is like its birth, you used to say, the death of the ocean is in the earth, you remember, Emmanuel? There are rivers that are white with the sediment that flows inside them, Emmanuel, there are animals that for days and nights won't take their eyes off the corpse.

No, said the big twin, it was before.

The little twin looked at her.

You're wrong, she said.

I'm not wrong, said the big twin.

The department head didn't hear. He asked what was before.

That Ma was killed, said the big twin.

Uncle Eliahu shifted nervously in his chair. He made a vigorous movement with his shoulders.

Why now? he said.

The big twin got hoarse, couldn't manage to hide the tinge of brutality in her voice. Of course it was before, she said.

The big twin—her name was Aya—and the little twin was Zaya, and Emmanuel said that in the five minutes between the birth of the one and the birth of the other was the whole alphabet, and since he said that, I haven't called them by their names, and really I don't know why, since Aya and Zaya are both after all nice enough names. The big twin said that in honor of Daddy she had put on her prettiest sweater, which he loved, and they made a tear in her prettiest sweater, which he loved.

Yes, said the curly-haired neighbor, with Mikela they made a tear in her cape.

Someone asked why.

Why what? said the big twin.

Why do they do the tearing?

The department head said it was written: "And he rent his garments," but really of course it was his soul that was rent.

The big twin asked why the clothes, why wasn't the soul enough.

The clothes remain torn, he said.

She laughed in a loud and strange voice.

What? she said.

She bit her lips, as if she was still hearing her own loud and strange laughter. You just don't wear them after that. That's all. What's left is the tear. You throw them out, she said.

In fact there are some people, said the curly-haired neighbor, who don't wear good clothes to a funeral. The man in the armchair grunted agreement and she said it again. Yes, there are some people who don't wear good clothes to a funeral, she said. The man in the armchair grunted again. He said the customs of mourning are wise customs, there's the week of mourning, and then the mourning month, and then the year. And the gravestone is put up on the thirtieth day, at the end of the month, it's time by then.

Yes, said Mikela, it's time.

The department head said it was based on the experience of generations, and therefore there was wisdom in it, he said that human experience is wisdom.

Of course, said Mikela.

The department head looked at her with obvious sympathy. I know, he said, but that's the way it is, that's the way it is, we have to accept the facts of life. He nodded his head. Besides, there's no choice.

Of course, said Mikela.

That's it, life goes on, what can you do, said the department head, looking at her with obvious sympathy.

Of course, said Mikela.

Uncle Eliahu got up suddenly as if a wind had blown him. He stood there looking around. Then he sat down all at once, the way he'd gotten up.

Geologists, the man in the armchair had started to say, and stopped, looking at Uncle Eliahu.

Geologists what? shouted Uncle Eliahu.

Mikela went over to him, stood there, but didn't say a word. Then she moved over to the man in the armchair, bent down and offered him the bowl of candied fruit.

It's fresh, she said. Then she bent over the curly neighbor, then bent over me.

It's fresh, she said. Her face was close to me now, the cheeks burning and the face cold, with the feverish pearly gleam in the skin of her face, and now, too, I was looking not at her but at the skin of her face. Again it seemed to me so cold that if it touched fire it would put it out. I took some candied fruit. She half-smiled and asked why I was looking at her like that. Oh, no, I said. The smile froze on her face, which was cold. I know, she said.

I don't know why I'm telling the details of the conversation, since really it isn't important and the story after all everyone knew, more or less, only in different versions, like any story in different accounts, and if it came to telling it in rough outline, it would go something like this, that one day Emmanuel asked her to sit down, asked Michelle, and said to her sit down Michelle, I have to talk to you, and he talked to her and said he hadn't known all those years that he didn't love her, simply hadn't known, and now that he'd tasted love, he couldn't give love up, and she said: Twenty years, twenty years? For twenty years you didn't

23
. . . .
The Letter That Came in Time

know, and she laughed, and after that said again: Twenty years twenty years you didn't know for twenty years, and laughed again, for twenty years you didn't know, she said, you didn't know for twenty years? And I won't keep you from love, she said, now that you've discovered love, I won't keep you from love after twenty years that you didn't know, twenty years without love, and they say she said all this while sitting on the chair and didn't get out of the chair from the moment he said: Sit down, Michelle, I have to talk to you, and only said twenty years twenty years, some people say she said that for an hour, some people say she said it all night and all the next nights only twenty years twenty years, and when he left she was still sitting on the chair and going on twenty years twenty years and after that he took his files and the notebooks and the papers and the shirts and they say that she even folded the shirts for him, buttoned, in a bundle, and after that she opened the doors of his closet again and left the doors open with the empty shelves, clean, and the hangers, and moved her chair over facing the closet. The doors were open, and she would bring her tea there and sit down, drinking, looking into the closet, and every week she would clean the shelves.

They remained friends. Sometimes he would phone. But he never came. It was hard for him to come, he said, and she said that was understandable, it was hard for him to come, she said. He of course didn't know the business about the closet, and maybe he'd have been angry if he had known. As I said, sometimes he would phone. The phone was on the table. She had a strong voice and she would talk into the receiver close and strong and look at the closet with the open doors and the shelves, and after a month or two or three, no one remembers exactly when and how it happened that she got into the car and started going on trips around the country and she said what she wants is trips around the country, that was always her dream, taking trips around the country, and on the road to Beersheba, halfway there, on the traffic island, she crashed. And Emmanuel, oh Emmanuel, and about this there are many versions, as usual, when he buried her, buried Michelle, the one he used to call Michellie, used to say: Is there anything to eat, Michellie? Why are you sad, Michellie? Her body was smashed. I wasn't at the funeral, but Zvi said they lowered in a little bundle, like a bundle of laundry.

After that it all went very quickly. The twins got married within a year, both of them, quickly, and they got pregnant, both of them, quickly, walked around together, pregnant, on the boulevard, bought apartments, quickly, bought furniture, and the young couple, the fresh couple, Mikela had an apartment here, facing this beautiful park on the boulevard and very quickly his books and his files and his notebooks and his typewriters piled up here.

The tall girl asked what about the geologists.

The department head was deep in thought. He said it was a great loss to the geologists. By the time a geologist like this develops, he said. After that he asked Mikela if she thought he'd known. Mikela didn't answer. And have you known for a long time? he said. She said yes, she'd known. The department head said she should be glad he hadn't suffered a lot. She said yes, she was glad. He asked if the disease had been brewing in him a long time. She said: It brewed, it brewed. The department head asked if there was anything he could do. No, there's nothing to do about it, she said. Her voice was quiet even now, and just a little muffled and sounded like out of a sack.

Just then the rain picked up all at once. It continued, heavy, like hail, with wild scrawls of lightning, and a blunt sound of thunder. You could hear cars skidding in the rain, and all at once, the way it started, it stopped, leaving a kind of dense clarity in the air. The man in the armchair said: It happens this time of year. Without a break, oddly, the light kept changing. One moment there was a lake of light on the house, sudden, then it quickly disappeared in a tangle of broken rays wheeling like birds with glittery wings over the boulevard in the wild sunset, and then evening fell strong and red and the street lights went on quickly, though the yard remained dark. Mikela put on the lights all over the house. There were lots of lamps there, hanging and on tables, and she went from lamp to lamp. It's nice, a lot of light, said the curly neighbor. Yeah, said the tall girl, like a celebration. Mikela kept moving around, flipping the switches. Then she went over to the big window and opened the curtain, and there was a pleasant dimness in the window, thick, purple, that spread, making a kind of channel.

The man in the armchair said he had to go, and so did the man in the rocking chair, and Mikela said thank you. He said the atmosphere had really been pleasant, and he admired that very much, how strong she was, and Mikela said thank you again, and said she would walk them outside, and Uncle Eliahu said: What's going to be with her? Aunt Eva, who hadn't made a remark the whole time, said there was nothing to worry about, that she's quiet, but Uncle Eliahu said he didn't like it so much that she was quiet, but just then Mikela came back. Seems she had really walked the guests out, because her dress was a little wet, sticking to her body, and she pulled it away a little from her body.

It keeps drizzling, she said, and the light at the entrance is burned out, have to change the bulb.

A nice man, said the curly neighbor.

Yes, said Mikela, a nice man.

You could see he felt good here, said the curly neighbor.

I hope so, I hope so, said Mikela.

You could see he thought a lot of Dad, said the big twin.

Of course, of course, said Mikela. Her hair was messed up from the wind outside, wrapped around her neck like a collar, and she pulled it together at the nape. Blotches of a sudden blush covered her face. It was tired, grey, and she took a long look at the big twin and then a long look at the little twin, and then again and it seemed to me she was also looking at me, though of course she didn't look at me, but you could definitely feel the zone of darkness in her eyes, she wasn't managing to see a straight line between her and whoever she was looking at, as if the room was empty, the center empty, as if someone was looking at her without her knowing it. There was a muffled noise like the distant wailing of cats at the window. She said: No, there are no cats here. Then she said: There are no dogs here, no jackals, not here in the wadi, that's a mistake. But the noise got louder and the mistake expanded. She said: Maybe it's the trees, they make noise at night, and she looked again at the big twin, and then at the little twin, and then again, pressing the palms of her hands against her body. They really looked hard, like two boards, and she said: It's the rain, what a wind there was. Her eyes darkened in a fog of tears and she quickly turned her head away. In the yard the light went on now and the window suddenly filled with light grey air, rising like the two halves of an opening bridge. What beautiful light, she said.

It was cold. I thought what are you supposed to say and maybe you're not supposed to say but still, you have to say something, but just then I heard her saying that in the next few days she would be very busy, since right after the week of mourning she was going to Paris, to her mother.

There was silence. The two twins turned red and Uncle Eliahu white. The tall girl, who broke the silence, said: That's right, that's what you should do, you're really smart. Someone asked if she was going for a long time. No, she said, and that she had to be back for the thirtieth, and before the thirtieth she had a lot of work, and I remember that she definitely used the word "work." The two twins asked what about the apartment. She said: I'm closing it up. They said maybe she should give them the key, and she said: No need. I'm back in a week. They were about to leave by then, and she said: Nothing to worry about, I'm coming back, the apartment is waiting for me here. Since there was silence, the tall girl said again: A good idea, taking a trip after the mourning week. And the curly neighbor also put a word in. Really, what are you going to sit around the house for, in any case he's not home, she said, and the other neighbor said: Who said he's not home? You couldn't tell if Mikela heard. She was standing in the middle of the room now, frozen, as if inside some artificial day leaning against an artificial door, the wet dress stuck to her body, her eyes not looking anywhere. Near her eyes she had little white patches of salt, and she looked like she wasn't seeing.

She shifted the belt of her dress a few times.

Nothing to worry about, she said, in a week I'm back, and she went over to the buffet. There were lots of ashtrays there full of butts and tobacco weed, and she moved the ashtrays aside a little and adjusted the position of the fossils, spacing them out across the buffet. They were full of bits of cookie and fruit and tobacco, and she passed her hand over the fossils, cleaning them a little, leaning over at the window, lingering, lingering, and when she straightened up, her head suddenly appeared disheveled and white in the rainy, streaming pane, like a head bobbing up out of the water. It's clearing up, she said.

The room was a mess, and everywhere there were stacks of cups with coffee dregs and bowls with leftover cookies and bits of fruit and rind and tail-ends of cigarettes and bits of tobacco on the tables and on the floor, and we said we'd straighten up a little, but she wouldn't let us. No need, she said, and repeated it: No need, I'm okay, in another hour everything will be clean and in order, and the curly neighbor said: He was right, the department head, you really are terrific, really strong. She said: Of course, of course, and even today the "of course" rings in my ears like a giant alarm bell, like an echo in a cave. I'm okay, really, she said quiet, very quiet, now without the pearly gleam on her face, which had become grey, the color of iron, and something like needles was flitting over her face, and that's the way she was a week later, when we went to the grave, and the next day she went off, with that iron color on her face, and the needles, and that's the way she came back a week later, in the same blouse and the same scarf and the same iron color on her face. She said she was glad she had gone to see her mother, it was the right thing at the right time, visiting her mother, and time was short and she had a lot to do, and she had to put the books in order, and the papers, and the fossils, had to put things in order, she said.

She didn't phone anyone, and we found out she was back only by coincidence, someone ran into her on the street and she said she was very busy, she had lots of work, lots of things to arrange before the thirtieth, it was hard to imagine how much there was to arrange before the thirtieth, she said. Of course no one asked what, and hardly anyone saw her after that, though the neighbors said that there were lights on until late at night and they heard her walking around in the apartment late at night.

For the thirtieth the gravestone was ready. The ceremony was short. She didn't ask people home. It's a mess at home, she said, so that from the cemetery everyone split up quickly. Now too her behavior was perfect, and she said she was glad she had managed to do everything and everything was going according to plan, and she hoped that's the way it would be in the days to come. The truth is the word "plan" sounded a little strange, but who paid attention to a little word by a fresh grave where they were putting up the stone.

The letter arrived three days later. It was a very short and simple letter, and it only said she hoped the letter would come on time, not too early and not too late, and that she'd planned everything just so, and there was a key under the rug at the entrance.

There really was a key under the rug. She was already cold. On the table there was a pad of paper precisely ruled, with numbers. At the bottom it said: What I wanted to leave to my mother I took with me when I visited her, so she already has it. On every object in the house there was a little sticker with a number, the way they do it on items in the stores, a number for the table and a number for the armchair and a number for the closet and a number for every book and every fossil and every ashtray and on the dresses and on the curtains. The digits were rounded and precise, the handwriting clear.

It said only that all the odd numbers were for Aya and the even numbers were for Zaya, and you could tell that she had put thought into every detail. The grey armchair was for Aya. The blue one was for Zaya. The white phone was for Aya. The one with the push-buttons was for Zaya. The dinner service for six with the flowers was for Aya. The one with the lines, for six, was for Zaya. The dog fossil with the snake's tail was for Aya. The one with the horse's head and the body like a handle was for Zaya. At the end of the page, down at the bottom, it said: With regard to the apartment, I transferred it to your names two months ago, so everything is in order. And then: The cash in the wallet is for me, for burial.

At the bottom it said: Regarding the typewriters, decide between you who gets the Hebrew and who gets the English, and maybe you should give both of them to Uncle Eliahu, who loves to type.

Translated by Marsha Pomerantz

hen I came in I heard her saying from the room: And three kilos of onions, don't forget. She must have been afraid he hadn't heard. Three kilos of onions, it's important, she repeated firmly. He was already in the corridor. Don't worry, everything will be all right, he replied from the corridor.

Inside the room lay B, dying. Attached to tubes, all wounded, all bandaged on the veins and arteries of her arms and legs. In the flushed, immobile face, swollen with cortisone, only the glittering little eyes darted.

I hope he won't forget anything, she said.

He won't forget, I said.

You'll come.

Of course, I said.

Mira will cook the meal.

Naturally, I said.

I've given instructions about everything.

Naturally, I said.

When my brother Nahum's wife died, she made him swear not to get married after her burial.

She made an effort to smile, but all you could see were her trembling, sensitive nostrils.

In my case Mira will cook the meal.

She made an effort to smile again.

She's a good cook.

I didn't know what to say. I felt her eyes fixed on my face, sharp and cold, like two steel nails.

Right after that I'll die, she said.

But B, I said.

The two steel nails turned red-hot.

Right after that I'll die. I'll hang on till Saturday.

Again she made an effort to smile.

I hope I'll hang on till Saturday.

Her eyes darted over me now, wild, as if she had four eyes.

I told him the exact menu. It has to be exact. It has to be just so.

I said of course it would be just so.

It has to be very delicious.

I said of course it would be very delicious.

I explained it to Alexander, she said, I explained that everything has to be just so.

He'll take care of it, I said.

Yes I hope he'll take care of it. All the time her eyes darted over me, wild. She said: The doctor's giving me two hours' leave. I can leave the hospital for two hours. I'll hang on for two hours.

Of course, I said.

He'll give me an injection first. And he'll come with me, of course. I invited him and his wife, of course.

I didn't ask her who else she'd invited. She waited.

There'll be ten, she said. Actually, eleven. And there'll be one empty place. I like one empty place.

Again she waited.

And Mira will serve the meal, of course.

I didn't know what to say. I remembered how when I was a child my mother once told me about plants that bled a red juice when they were broken. She said: I explained to her exactly how to set the table.

Now too I didn't know what to say. She said: The injection will be enough for two hours. At four I have to be back here.

I told her that she would be back here on time.

Yes, I'll be back here on time, she said.

I didn't know what to say. There was silence.

And that's it, she said.

There was silence.

After that, that's it, she said.

There was silence.

You don't know what to say, she said. There was silence. It was evident that she felt confined inside her skin. She said: After that, that's it. And next week—she tried to move her head, which was heavy, and it was evident that she felt more and more confined inside her skin.

Everything will be settled quickly, she said.

I didn't ask what.

Her eyes darted over me again, rapacious, and I could feel the hot mud in her body.

Yes, everything will be settled quickly, she said and sank her head into the pillow as if there was an abyss of air there inside the pillow.

I looked at her swollen, exhausted face. Her chin was bandaged, and I thought about the place where the animal's neck begins. I thought about the bones, the hair and the teeth. Her eyes ran over me so wild that for a moment I thought that she heard through her eyes. There was a pearl hanging on her chest. She said: I explained to her exactly how to lay the table. She breathed heavily. She said: You see, you turn into a watchdog.

Everything, like death itself, was clear and absolute. It was clear that she had taken care of everything, including what would happen afterwards. Unlike death it was clear that this too was planned. Suddenly I saw her strolling down the avenue with a white parasol. She said: I brought it from Japan but I look like a little Chinese woman. She had a sly laugh. She really did look like a little Chinese woman, strolling in the shade in the cypress avenue with a white parasol. I remembered the amusing stories of her travels, when she traveled round the world with Alexander, round the world more than once. It seemed to me that she was searching for a mirror, that she was avid to see her face in the mirror. Again I remembered the story of the mandrake plant that screamed when it was pulled up and how my mother told me that its root was black when it was pulled up. I looked at her wounded swollen veins, and although she was all covered up I felt as if she saw through her whole body.

You can't get that thought out of your blood, she said.

She was very quiet now, as protected as possible inside the pillow. She told me everything quietly, dryly. She told me how she intended to set the table, who would sit next to whom, and which table-napkins she had given instructions to take from the cupboard and where they were in the cupboard and under what. Which dinner service was to be used to serve the meal on and which to serve the coffee afterwards, what to make the compote from and in what bowl, and to take out the cutlery with the long white wooden handles and not to forget mustard seeds, it was very nice to put mustard seeds in a salad. Afterwards she explained what kind of soufflé she intended making, and the quantities of courgettes, garlic and onion, and that she had asked Alexander to make sesame sweets. He is a great expert at sesame sweets. He enjoys making sesame sweets very much. There was nothing he liked better than making sesame sweets. The bandages on her arms were stained red and she looked as if she were simultaneously draining blood and words out of herself.

Enough, I said.

She didn't hear.

He's a great expert at sesame sweets, she said.

Enough, I said.

She said: And I asked him to make sugar beet soup. Everybody likes sugar beet soup. It's a pretty color, sugar beet soup.

She was speaking now neither quickly nor slowly. Her face was exhausted and only her eyes burned with the force of hostile nature.

I asked if you liked sugar beet soup, she said.

A sudden cold blew from her, as if the fever had chilled her. She wiped her mouth with the tail end of a bandage and sat up slightly. Again it seemed to me that she was searching for a mirror, that she was avid to see her face in the mirror.

I haven't got one on me, I said in alarm.

She asked what.

What? she said obstinately.

I said I liked sugar beet soup.

She looked at me and with one hand hit the iron bed, which made a sound like a musical stone. She kept cruelly silent.

It's good, especially in summer, I said.

She kept cruelly silent.

I'm talking nonsense, I said.

She continued to keep cruelly silent. You thought I wanted a mirror, she said. No, I don't need a mirror.

She moved the infusion, holding her only luggage in her hand.

I'm glad you came to see me, she said. Yes, I'm certainly glad you came to see me. There was a kind of deep biological insult in her voice. She turned towards me, trying to smile.

Yes, it's good in summer, sugar beet soup, she said. Again she tried to smile. Her voice choked and quivered and she swallowed her voice and looked at me quivering from the depths of the pillow.

I feel it approaching, she said.

I didn't know what to say.

It approaches in broad daylight, she said, it will come next week.

She wept silently.

Not like a thief in the night, in broad daylight, she said.

I didn't know what to say. She wept silently. Her face was flooded, and it was hard to tell if it was wet with tears or sweat. She looked so small now in the bed among the pillows, sunk into them as if in a narrow mountain pass, waving with the infusion in her hand, making an effort to open her arms and able to move only in one direction, like a bird capable of flying only in one direction. I thought: You can't get that thought out of your blood, that's what she said. I'm talking nonsense, that's what she said. The strong women, the strong women, I thought. My clever friend B, I thought. I didn't know what to say. I asked myself how many stones made a pile.

I definitely want it to be very festive, she said.

It was very festive. We arrived at one o'clock precisely. The other guests also arrived at one o'clock precisely. The table was punctiliously laid. I counted: There were eleven places. Everything was especially gay. The napkins were brightly colored and flowered with little bouquets of little flowers clustered in tiny little goblets. At the door Mira received the guests. She was wearing a black dress with black lace, she had soft fair skin and the black lace emphasized her fair skin and the sympathetic melancholy of soft skin.

They'll be here soon, she said. Her face was tense and she made an effort to disguise the embarrassment in her voice. She said that there had been a problem finding something for B to wear and Alexander had driven to the hospital three times and three times she had sent him back to change the dress. One of the times she had asked for the gold sari-dress Alexander had brought her from India and then she had sent the gold sari-dress back. She said she had returned it because of the buttons that weren't properly sewn and they would open during the feast and instead of occupying herself with the guests she would be occupied with the buttons, and Alexander said: That's better, that's better, imagine her sitting there in the gold sari-dress, and it rustles too, Mira said, and they brought her the wide floral dress.

A faint blush appeared on her cheeks as she said this. I hope she'll be pleased with what I sent, she said and added that it really was very difficult, because B was very bloated. She spoke carefully, with the same sympathetic melancholy that added charm to her voice and she was incorrigibly sympathetic too when we heard the sound of the car approaching and when we heard it entering the yard and Alexander thundering: There, we made it, you see.

It must have seemed a little strange when we all formed up in a row. There was silence. She got out slowly and approached slowly. The doctor supported her on one side and Alexander on the other, and she walked silently down the long green garden path with her eyes making a big circle that instantly swallowed up all of us standing in a row. She smiled.

We're lucky it's a nice day, she said. She was wearing her jewelry and her eyes stood out in her face like big brightly colored glass beads.

Wonderful, thundered Alexander, you see. There was a dead cigar butt in his mouth and his breathing was loud and excited. He was a big man with long legs and big steps and he always had magnificent wooden boxes full of big cigars.

I told you it would be a lovely day, he beamed.

She didn't look at him and only swallowed us all up as if we were some kind of shapeless stain. Then she took a small step forward. Then she took another step forward.

Truly, what luck, a lovely day, she confirmed.

You see, thundered Alexander.

She took another small step forward. Her head was heavy and she stepped carefully onto the lawn with one foot and then stepped carefully with the other foot as if there were land mines on the lawn. Her bowed head betrayed the thin deleted hair and the ominous bald spots. She raised it, stretched, and hit her body with both hands. There was a metallic sound and I saw her standing in the gold sari-dress that Alexander had brought her from India with the power of a short queen who had lost her kingdom but not her authority. And she set off on her race, the strong sick mare.

You mowed the lawn in my honor, she said.

In my childhood, in Nesher, I once saw a huge rock torn from the mountain. First it crumbled slowly, for days, maybe for a year, maybe for generations. When it fell it wasn't rock any more. It only looked like one. In reality it was crumbs of soil.

But in my childhood in Nesher it hung huge in the air on the mountain and I thought that it was holding the mountain up. One day, at noon, in summer, when the sun on the mountain blazed and the rock was all gold like my friend B in the gold sari-dress she wasn't wearing, suddenly the rock tore. But in my childhood in Nesher it was still hanging there for years in the air holding up the mountain and at noon I would look for it on top of the mountain whirling and crumbling in the air all summer, and it seems to me the summer after that too. Afterwards came the winter and I asked myself how long it took for a mass of rock hanging on the mountain to fall off the mountain and I asked myself what material it was that held grain to grain and sometimes I remembered that when it fell I was afraid that the sun had fallen. Every day I looked at the quarry then.

The table, the table, said my friend B. This was after she had already crossed the lawn, still stepping on it with small careful steps, as if there were shoe mines on the lawn. By then she had already extricated herself from the support of the doctor and the support of her husband, leaving the two embarrassed men behind her and us behind her as she proceeded alone along the narrow path, advancing with a tremendous effort forward into the house, her house. Her hands were limp, exposed, and again she beat them like two wings against the two sides of her body as she approached the door and stood for a moment on the threshold and then entered with a sudden decision with a strong movement of a person setting out in stormy weather. It was hot. Her face was flushed. But it gave off a chill that was hard to bear.

Wonderful, she said.

She said this three times, in the same tone, but each time the temperature changed and the chill grew more unbearable, as if with each statement something was happening in her body. After that her eyes narrowed and she looked only at the table. Now she stood alone, apart from everyone else. She drew herself up a little, exhausted, and her eyes darted low, narrowed on the table. Everything was green. Everything was a lie. And she stood there, as if in the gold sari-dress, apart from everyone else, and there was no way either good or bad. And only everything was green everything was a lie. And apart from everyone else she began to walk towards the table as in ancient times those sentenced to die walked towards the hills.

Wait, raged Alexander.

Wonderful, she said.

She turned towards us, her confused audience.

Really, they've made it look wonderful, no? she said.

Her sick eaten body was already stretched as far as an eaten body could go and she stretched it further and further and further her eyes on every single one of us still standing there in that miserable row. And everything was green. Everything was a lie. And all that existed was only the chasm between one look and the next and one moment and the next and the passion and power that she now possessed.

She smiled.

She had a blue shadow under her eyes, and the smile took its time passing from one eye to the other.

Really, they've made it look wonderful, no? she said, drugged and poisoned, with the eyes of a she-wolf.

She knew the price of the performance.

Really, they've made it look wonderful, no? she said exultantly.

She spoke slowly and it took time for her to get from word "a" to word "b," from place "a" to place "b," and the only thing she didn't have was time.

She knew that too.

The table really did look wonderful. It was covered with a red woven cloth with airy stripes woven into the cloth, so that the color of the wood of the table showed through it. There were eleven places round the table, eleven little straw baskets for bread, and eleven slender-legged glasses, white garlands engraved around their rims, eleven tumblers of Hebron glass in purple, green and blue and a khaki color for cold drinks. In the center stood a huge glass jug with a silver handle and silver tongs and a heap of little square cubes of ice, and flat round slices of lemon floating in the water, and another eleven tumblers of low Hebron glass with a few low flowers stuck loosely in each of them to look like bunches of wild flowers dotted about, and then there was the dinner service, not the splendid one used for formal occasions, but the pseudo-simple, pseudo-crude one used by the family, a clay service in a clay color with a narrow brown stripe encircling the plates like a slender ring, and of course there was the cutlery with the long white wooden handles. The table was ready for the feast. On every clay plate stood a little clay plate and on it an artichoke, and scattered about the table stood saucers of a lemon and dill sauce for dipping. The wine bottles stood on a little table next to the main table, in front of the window, and there were plenty of salt cellars, pepper pots and rolled-up napkins.

She was still standing at the door, flushed, examining the intricate colorful setting, which really was magnificent. Suddenly she took a small step forward, then she approached the table and stood there for a moment in agitation, and then she said that you don't put red table-napkins

on a red tablecloth and she had specifically asked for the antique-rose damask set. Alexander apologized and came back with the antique-rose
damask set. She said: You put table-napkins in rings, don't you know
that you put table-napkins in rings, what, didn't Mira remember? I specifically asked for it, she said. Alexander brought a pile of narrow wooden
rings and inserted each napkin into a ring and she circled the table with
little steps and examined the cards and the names on the plates. It'll do,
she said, and after that Alexander's voice rose thunderously and he called
the guests in from the garden to the feast. B sat in her usual place, opposite the window. Opposite her sat Alexander, with his back to the window. Mira sat next to him as the guest of honor of the meal. They began
with chilled wine. Alexander asked everyone what wine. There was Ver-
mouth, a dry white wine and a rosé. B said: I want some too. Alexander
fumed that it wasn't allowed. The doctor said nothing.

It's allowed, she insisted.

I knew it, he whispered angrily.

Full, she said exultantly.

Her eyes were bulging and she tried to make her voice sound gay.

Full, full, she said exultantly. She raised the glass carefully and set it
down carefully.

In vain I try to remember what was said, I can't, but I remember exactly what we ate and even what every dish looked like, the color, the
quantities and the combinations, the gleam of the cutlery and the gleam
of the glasses, and from which side they began serving in what order
and what. There was nothing out of the ordinary during the meal,
everyone kept to the unwritten contract and nobody knew, or remembered or saw. B sat next to me, speaking now too neither quickly nor
slowly, but laughing very slowly, with a kind of hidden violence, and it
was clear that the same program would go on running till the end of the
meal and in this wretched lost battle all the data were positive, there was
all the time in the world and in endless directions. She let this be understood with every look, throwing out short, packed sentences, gulping
water, jealously guarding the next wave of words. Her hands were
wounded, and she made efforts to hide her wounded hands, trying to
eat bunched up and move her fingers as little as possible. She tore off
the artichoke leaves and dipped them in the lemon and dill sauce, and
seated at the head of the table, at the most convenient vantage point,
she didn't miss a move made by anyone. They said what a pleasant
breeze. There really was a pleasant breeze. They said what a delicious

sauce. The sauce really was delicious. After that they served the soup and she said to Alexander that she would dish up, put the tureen next to her. To my surprise it wasn't sugar beet soup. It was consommé. She smiled, inclining her head slightly in my direction, and it seemed to me that we both understood the code. The tremendous difficulty was the words. Today I'm not so sure about it anymore, returning to the handsome dining room with the big wide windows, the bright locks of light and my friend B sitting there wearing her jewels and sweating under her jewels. She shifted them from place to place on her neck, and today when I read a little book about birds I remembered her, my friend B sitting burning, with drooping shoulders and swollen hands, like a bird feeding on its own blood.

Consommé, excellent, she said.

She laughed.

There's nothing like hot soup on a hot day. She laughed again. Alexander, the ladle, please. We'll begin at the end, Mira's first.

She said this slowly, quietly, and smiled a little smile, as if the fact that they had changed the soup made her feel especially gay. Then she sank the ladle into the middle, making a little whirlpool in the center, in the middle of the tureen, holding onto it hard, as if she were holding a heavy wooden stick in her hand. Her eyes bulged, glassy, two balls of celluloid, which did not move, fixed on the ladle, their gleam getting duller from minute to minute, and you could feel how from minute to minute, together with the cancer, the hatred of strangers bloomed in her body.

It's important to mix it well, to get the "heart of the soup" into every plate, she said, and we'll begin at the end, Mira's first. She smiled a little smile again. Her forehead was bathed in sweat and she wiped her forehead.

Suddenly it's grown hotter, she said with the same little smile looking round the table from one to the next and suddenly she began to count aloud.

Don't worry, there'll be second helpings, she said and drew the tureen towards her, trying to increase the gaiety in her voice.

Overenthusiasm is weakness, writes Tolstoy in *War and Peace*, but my friend B, for all her cleverness, trapped in a narrow strip of life, for this one hour at noon, forgot, feeling, for this one hour at noon, her old power, trying, for this one hour at noon, to remove some misunderstanding as she ladled the consommé with her forehead bathed in sweat, and she wiped it away making the same movement over and over again but it kept on coming back. Her face was alternately red and white, and she dished the soup out slowly, plate after plate, stirring it with the ladle after every plate to make sure that everyone would get the "heart of the soup," and everyone around the table held out his hand with the empty plate and then drew back his hand with the full plate and smiled and said: Thank you, you're wonderful, and she said: Marvelous, and everyone around the table knew that it was murder, the disease had murdered her body.

They ate and talked and ate and talked again. Someone said he had bought a movable air conditioner and that a movable air conditioner was a wonderful thing, and someone said that he hated movable things, he liked things fixed to the wall. After that they talked about how Haifa had become a dirty town. Someone remarked that it had never been clean and it had only had the reputation of being a clean town, and after that as usual they asked why we were still living in Hadar instead of moving up to the Carmel, there was nothing left in Hadar but for lawyers and prostitutes, and she said with a laugh that she knew Zvi would say that of the two he preferred the prostitutes, and she agreed with him, but at that moment precisely a wind sprang up and he asked something about the poplar.

It will have to be pulled up, said Alexander.

Someone asked why.

Alexander said that it would raise the house.

Someone asked how a poplar could raise a house.

Alexander explained that it had long roots and it could raise a house.

A house? the doctor asked.

Alexander explained that its roots were so long that they destroyed the foundations from inside the ground. The house remains whole but it has no foundations, it has nothing to stand on, it falls down whole, do you understand?

Strange, said the doctor.

Why? said B. She was apparently in pain. She smiled. And it never stops shedding its leaves. It always seems that it's going to be left naked.

The doctor sipped his soup.

Yes, he said, growth.

B turned towards him, leaned over to the middle of the table and took the salt cellar.

It has to be strong, it acts as a wind-break, she said.

A wind-break? said the doctor.

She went on playing with the salt cellar.

It has scars on its leaves. When the wind goes through it whistles.

It wasn't clear what the connection was, and she repeated: It has scars on its leaves. Haven't you noticed that it whistles? There was passion in her voice. She said: I'm very fond of the whistling.

You're tiring yourself for nothing, said Alexander.

She put the salt cellar down immediately and pushed it to the center of the table.

Yes, I'm tiring myself for nothing, she said, and she picked up the salt cellar again and put it down again on the red tablecloth. Then she paused in order to gain control of her voice.

Her face blazed.

The tamarisk tree has leaves with salt nodules.

Her face blazed even more.

Didn't you know that the tamarisk has leaves with salt nodules, didn't you know? It's doomed to die in the desert, she said. She asked if anyone had heard of the Dead Sea apple, the apple of Sodom. Haven't you heard of the apple of Sodom? The apple of Sodom, she repeated, and Hell, haven't you heard of Hell? There are lots of synonyms for Hell, didn't you know? And the apple of Sodom, nobody's heard of it, nobody knows?

She laughed again. She had strong teeth when she laughed.

Once people believed that there was an animal that breathed forever. Alexander, what's the name of the animal? They cut off its head, you know, and it goes on breathing after they've cut off its head.

We're in the middle of eating, Alexander thundered.

Oh, I forgot, we're in the middle of eating, I apologize.

Her face was full of blood. I forgot, we're in the middle of eating. I certainly do apologize. She held onto her hands, which were trembling hard, as if an electric shock had passed through her body. And a table like this too, with one's husband and one's best, one's dearest friends. She looked around her, unable to control her hands. Really, the best and dearest, I really do apologize.

You're going too far, Alexander thundered.

Yes, I'm going too far, I'm definitely going too far, she said. She said this now in a dry, matter-of-fact tone, and she still couldn't control her hands. And the table-napkin, Alexander they're the old-rose damask table-napkins you know. It's my memory, you know, I've simply forgotten the animal's name.

Instead of eyes, under the forehead, her two celluloid balls bulged, blank, glassy, a foreign body in her face. Again she tried to make her voice sound gay.

You can serve the salads now, she announced, tugging at the wide flowery dress that revealed ravaged shoulders, all bones, the arms hanging from them as if they came from some other place. I read this week, I don't remember where, that ever since 1945 the world had lost its stability.

Since '45? Alexander inquired.

Yes, since '45, she said.

Why since '45 precisely? asked Alexander.

It's a fact that the world really has lost its stability. But nobody knows yet what the attributes of the new, unstable material are, she said.

The two celluloid balls suddenly raced feverishly round.

And it can be anybody, she said. She spoke as if her voice had been wounded. Materials engineering, it's a complicated business, she said.

Suddenly she raised her back, tilted her body backwards and pressed hard against the back of the chair, raising her head too as she looked hopelessly in front of her for a moment, wringing her hands. You can't live outside your home, that's what it is, I think that that's what it is, she said suddenly and straightened violently as if she wanted to increase the volume of air around her. She was breathing fast, and I thought that pain, like fire, reduplicated itself in the process of burning. She kept on wringing her hands. It's a cannibalistic thing, she once said to me. Living inside a sack, she once said to me. And all the time the leaves are rustling, she said.

She was still sitting erect like a dog.

The poplar had a concert voice, she said.

Around the table there was a sudden stir.

I've already said that I have great difficulty in remembering what was said during the meal, and yesterday I called someone to ask. She didn't remember either nor did her husband. They only remembered that nothing special happened until someone mentioned Beilinson Hospital, and B said: No, I'm not going to Beilinson. Alexander said that no one wanted her to go to Beilinson and she went on looking at her plate. Alexander said that she wouldn't even go into a street called Beilinson. Her face was full of blood now too. She bent over and began sipping the soup with small sips and said into the soup that nobody was going to call a street after her. Alexander shouted, but she didn't raise her face from the soup and said that that was what she wanted, not to have a street called after her. You'll be able to walk freely in all the streets, she said. Alexander hastily removed the napkin from his knees. He stood up, but she went on eating her soup. Like mountaineers, advancing by stages, she said into her soup. Then I didn't yet know the story and I only understood later that people, like history, repeat themselves. It was told to me years later, on the telephone from Haifa to Tel Aviv. The lines were busy and I couldn't hear very clearly. The doctor joked that it wasn't so easy to get a street named after you. B didn't hear. She ordered the meat and salads to be brought but before that for Alexander to tell the story about the cobra. They all knew the story about the cobra but they all liked the story about the cobra too, and he lit a cigar, drew a breath and loudly and lustily recounted what he had already loudly and lustily recounted dozens of times before, how he had brought this cobra back with him from the UN Conference to the Tel Aviv zoo on the plane in a suitcase, and how over the ocean the cobra had escaped from the suitcase. It was night time. The passengers were sleeping. And when he opened the suitcase it was empty. And he drew a breath and went on telling how he had closed the suitcase, already knowing that the cobra was taking a walk over the ocean between the seats in the plane, and on all the seats people were sound asleep in the plane, and he drew a breath again and stretched his long strong legs, settling back in his chair, and she looked at him, her eyes concentrating more and more on one point of his face as she tapped her plate with the tip of her fork like background music accompanying his loud voice. You could see how her eyes grew smaller and smaller, narrowing on a smaller and smaller point of his face, moving along some strange, slanting, oblique line and after that this same oblique line moved around the table, passing glassily from plates to faces and faces to plates and together with it moved a faint little smile, but it was impossible to tell to which side.

You can serve the meat, she said.

The oblique line now moved onto Mira.

On the big wooden platter, she said and averted her face with the movement of a person crossing to the opposite pavement. I hope the color has been preserved, she said, cooking ruins the colors. She breathed hard. Have you noticed, most vegetables go red when they're cooked, have you noticed? She breathed hard again. The vegetable peel, it's all in the vegetable peel, she said, looking for words, but the words didn't meet, like objects that don't belong to each other. You never know how materials will behave, she said. She laughed a little. I like this dinner service, this clay one, she said.

Mira scattered the salads over the table (I've already said that there were mustard seeds). Then she served the soufflé and the quiche and a variety of baked goods, and added ice cubes to the beautiful jug for cold water. There was red cabbage cooked in wine, a dish of tiny onions in wine (a delicacy of which B was particularly fond), sweet and sour beetroot, and green beans with almonds. After that a magnificent platter arrived with a magnificent crown of rice decorated with mushrooms and almonds and raisins and thin slices of crystallized fruit. In the end came the meat, a huge joint lying on a thick board of pale wood and surrounded by pieces of chicken cooked in orange juice and wine. Alexander began to carve the meat and he asked us all what we wanted and B said that Alexander was a master meat-carver and all the time she followed his movements and looked at him. The inner meat, the inner meat, please, she said and all the time she looked at him, and all of us knew that she was the one who took care of everything for him including the woman who would take her place, and she was the one who had brought her into the house, taught her the dishes he liked and how he liked his shirt collars ironed. And she had learnt quickly. She had soft graceful steps and she passed round the table with the salad bowls and dished up with soft graceful steps, and after that she brought potatoes in aluminum foil with cream sauce and put them in the center of the table and as she walked she bent over and the doctor asked if there was garlic in it. B said: Yes, there's garlic in it and so what if there's garlic in it? Today I'm eating garlic too today I'm omnipotent and she asked Mira to bring the peach melba and the apricot whip and the iced soufflé, and Mira went into the kitchen a few times with soft graceful steps and piled the peach melba and the iced lemon soufflé and the apricot whip in an exquisite black dish on the table and all the time B looked at the table and where she put everything down on the table and then someone suggested drinking a toast to her and everyone stood up and drank a toast to her and she stood up and drank too. Her face was still flaming and you could feel the heat of her breath burning her.

We can begin the meat, she said.

She exhorted them not to forget the gravy and said that Alexander always forgot the gravy. Afterwards she said that the gravy was out of this world and suggested that after the meal we should all tell a story and Alexander would be first. He asked which one.

The one about the cobra.

There was silence.

The one about the cobra, everyone likes the story about the cobra, she said.

There was silence.

Why not? said the doctor.

She laughed a nervous laugh.

I forgot, you already told it, she said.

I can tell it twice, why not? Alexander thundered.

Certainly, you can tell it twice, she said. Her voice sounded hoarse, like a sad croak, and she looked at him now, very concentrated, in the way a person might look at a point in a flashlight.

Never mind, she said.

The arteries in her neck suddenly filled with blood and she bent down and held the nape of her neck as if her neck was broken.

The meal, as usual, took longer than expected and I saw the doctor stealing a glance at his watch. She must have seen too, because she turned to me and raised her hand, making a sign with her hand. No, the two hours aren't over yet, she said and went on staring distantly at her hand, as if it were the hand of some other body, and to this day her voice runs after me through the years: No, the two hours aren't over yet, and packed into this brief statement, like gunpowder, lay the entire foreseeable future. Her breathing was rapid, her eyelids pink, and she was already playing her role with only partial success, failing to fill in the gaps. After we finished eating she announced that for coffee and the sesame sweets we would move to the living room, and that Alexander had, indeed, made sesame sweets. He adored making sesame sweets. Here too everything was ready and waiting. There were eleven seats, a lot of little tables and a lot of bunches of flowers. The window was open, high, wide, and it was possible to see the sea from end to end, limitlessly. B sank into an armchair, slowly, laboriously, supporting one hand with the other. Then she relaxed her wrist, this too slowly and laboriously, as if it was the hardest thing in the world to relax her wrist. Suddenly she looked exhausted. Instead of the flush there were little brown spots on her face, like flakes of rust, and every time I remember that picture I think that there are machines that can withstand field conditions but not transport conditions. And moving into the living room, ah no, with that my friend B could not cope, and how she got there making her head move and her hands move, advancing as if she were swimming by means of a strong backwards motion, and I said to myself something about the heavy soul in the light shell, I caught myself thinking: A deciduous tree, the poplar tree, I remembered the leaves with the salt nodules and how she said: The inner meat, the inner meat, please, and he said: But what do you want, and she said: My strength, I want my strength, and he said: What side should I begin on, and she said: The green-blue light the blue-green ray, the laser is a weapon that blinds, she said. Everyone remembers windows, doors, she said, everyone knows only a few details, the body is a particularly deep grave, she said, brushing crumbs off the old-rose damask napkin, and I wish you all a pleasant day, she said, and to this day I cannot remember the second incident and only that a wind began to blow, the huge poplar trembled and a whistling sound came from the poplar and the table rose and the tablecloth rose and the doors and the glasses and the chairs and the bottles and the antiques rose and my friend B remained sitting there next to an empty table in an empty room of a house being raised by a poplar tree.

Suddenly she said: Wait a minute, first Alexander has to bring the sesame. He hasn't brought the sesame yet. We forgot the sesame.

She laughed. As I said before, she had strong teeth when she laughed.

Everything's fading out like in the movies, she said.

I didn't know what to answer and I smiled and she looked at me and to this day I can't forget the way she looked at me. Then she turned her head ninety degrees and looked at me again. Her face was strange now as if it was cut in half and like you sometimes see in the movies as if she had two faces one on the other and she no longer wanted to remove the second layer before the first. These faces were now facing me fully, two faces one on the other in two silhouettes with thick contours. It seemed to me that she was still trying to hide the fear but not the poisoned life, and that it was impossible to stand it for one more minute and I saw her suddenly bending the upper half of her body forward so hard that it

46

seemed to me that the fear was cutting her in half like a butcher's knife. But she didn't say a word. One contour was distorted and underneath it a contour with strong teeth laughed. Again it seemed to me that it was impossible to stand it for one more minute but she stood it. We all sat and she stood. She even straightened up, stretched her neck and looked round for a minute at everyone sitting there with a soft look, a look like shot silk.

I'd like to hear a violin, she said.

We can put on a record, said Alexander.

No, a live violin, she said.

There was silence. Her glance strayed round the seated square with a circular movement, one by one, with the face that recalled her face, its intelligence, and with the two contours that ran over it wildly with the tremendous desire to live. We were still sitting and she stood, looking at the tables and the cupboards and the antiques (I remembered how conscientiously she used to dust them) and all the fixed and the moving objects and the dozens of different signposts of time scattered here as if they were things forgotten somewhere by mistake.

Yes, a live violin, to see the fingers on the strings, she said.

Her look suddenly grew vague.

I'd like to hear a live violin, she repeated staring in front of her frozenly. Even her eyelids didn't move and it was clear that everything was behind her everything was over, existing in some distant time, old and buried, and only that tremendous desire to live was streaming through her arteries like a powerful shot of morphine.

She selected words as if they were precision instruments.

I stood up before the coffee because I wanted to say something.

Her face turned a silver shade.

My plan was —

Enough, roared Alexander.

She looked at him with a desperate squint, shifted from one foot to the other and swaying slightly pressed both hands tightly to her body, as if she were wearing a straitjacket.

My plan was —

I don't agree, roared Alexander.

She shifted from one foot to the other again, and the red blotches returned to her face and one eye suddenly grew black and swollen with a bruise under the eye. She looked as if she had been given a punch in the eye.

My plan was—she began again, but the words came out of her mouth strangely as if they were going in the opposite direction, from the mouth to the heart, and had disintegrated on the way.

She began again: My plan was—

In a story, as in life itself, there's a moment when it seems unreal to die in the middle of summer, forever. It's tremendously hard to bear the continuing dryness in the mouth, the burning in the feet, but it's unreal to think that suddenly thoughts stop and a human being turns into a corpse. But perhaps B was not concerned with all this. She was poisoned with morphine, her time was running out and she still wanted to say something. Again she shifted from one foot to the other, her one eye grew increasingly black increasingly swollen and her skin and her face were now completely opaque and their color made you think of a material resembling coral.

She looked very exhausted but nobody dared stand up and the doctor didn't tell her to sit down either, and she stood there, with her one black eye, shifting from foot to foot, the other eye glittering big and open devouring the trees and the windows and the rays of light in the windows, unbelievably bright, transparent, endless, penetrating the surface of the skin without leaving a scar.

Nobody dared get up and the doctor didn't tell her to sit down either, and she went on standing and looking and seeing and looking, not moving, unblinking. It was hot. The poplar whistled. She made a strange movement with her head, the eye with the black bruise fixed on the poplar, the other eye in some other place low down on the trunk, as if she were trying to separate the shape from the background or the treetop from the ground. It seemed as if she were looking not at the objects but at the margins of the objects and everything looked really huge, really tiny, really split-second. Again she strayed over the faces of the seated people with staring eyes. Time passed. More time passed. And I saw her strolling to and fro along the long veranda opposite the poplar tree in the way you sometimes clearly see people you once knew in places where they have never been at all.

Have you ever looked at a plant after it has been chopped down or after a fire and what happens to the bitter hairy poisonous fruit? Have you ever looked at the hard round seed and what happens to the hard round seed? The fruit of the birch tree for example is ground up. Ground up it's used for rat poison or for spraying fish. Have you ever seen a bare tree blossoming? The tree shines, naked, pink, even the trunk is visible in the distance so pink and shining it is in its beautiful blossoming. Some people say it's the tree on which Judas was hanged after he betrayed Christ. Others say it was used to crucify Christ. Since no material is ever lost in the world perhaps a bit of it is still hanging on a tree somewhere and has become part of the naked trunk or the beautiful blossoming.

She turned to Alexander again, squinting desperately, and you could feel the wild cat bursting from her body.

My plan was—

Instead of contracting into a ball with pain, her body expanded and she opened her fingers, still able to fly, but they were heavy, swollen, made more of lead than blood, and she dropped them and remained standing for a long time without moving.

My plan was—for each and every one of the people sitting here— who are all very dear to me—she took a breath—to say one sentence to me—she took a breath—and also—

She took a breath.

My plan was—to tell each and every one of the people sitting here— who are all very dear to me—she took a breath—what role they played in my life—she took a breath—but it's impossible—it's impossible.

She took a breath.

It's impossible, I can't do it.

She took a breath.

In any case, I have to go, time's up, she said.

Her face was wet and she wiped it with her hand, like a little girl.

And in any case I'm burning, I'm on fire, she said and wiped her face with her hand, like a little girl.

When she was standing in the door she stopped suddenly, and turned round.

I'm sorry we didn't drink the coffee, she said, you'll have to drink it without me. Mira will serve the sesame and the cake.

In the middle, when she entered the living room, there was another incident that I forgot to tell and skipped over. It was before she collapsed into the armchair. She asked Zvi to sing her a song. He asked what song.

Never mind, whatever you want, she said, and unable to keep standing she fell into the armchair. He knelt at her feet and began to sing:

> Seven mice and a mouse
> Are eight I suppose
> So I take my chapeau
> And say goodnight.

She didn't move. Her hands trembled on her knees. They were cold and damp and stuck to her knees like clamps. She hummed:

> Seven mice and a mouse
> Are eight I suppose
> So I take my chapeau
> And I say goodnight
> I take my chapeau
> And off I go
> Where can you go so late at night
> All on your own.

A week later, on Saturday, we were there in the garden and there were a lot of other people there too who had come to condole with Alexander. He came up to us and stood with us for a moment next to the poplar tree.

I don't want you to hear it from strangers, he said, Mira's living here.

We didn't know what to say.

I thought you realized, he said. A strange smile crossed his face.

That's why she had the feast.

We didn't know what to say. Zvi mumbled something. Then he said he would go and get us something to drink and I said: All right, I'll wait here, and I stood and looked at the beautiful garden and the beautiful woman moving round serving fruit and lemonade and iced coffee. Among the other antiques and jars and capitals there was a sarcophagus that I forgot to mention, made of wonderful white stone, standing open in the garden and my friend B would sometimes sit on its rim as if it were a bench. I couldn't resist the temptation and I sat down on it too as if it were a bench and looked at the beautiful woman moving round there in the garden and she suddenly seemed to me like a small detail of no significance in the whole story, moving round the garden with little steps as if she had been moving round here all along. I've already said that she had a soft walk and a soft neck and I saw him standing in the kitchen passing his hand over her soft neck and I said to Zvi, let's go home. He said: Yes, let's go home. The poplar made a loud concert sound and on the bench sat my friend B. On the other side of the bench. Her black eye had disappeared and her eyes were china blue, a warm blue, sparkling on the rim of the sarcophagus, and inside it her head swayed like a giant marionette beating the stone of the sarcophagus. I was very tired. I said to Zvi, let's go home. He said: Yes, let's go home.

When we left he asked if I remembered what she had said.

I asked what.

Translated by Dalya Bilu

This week, when I finally left the Haifa apartment, I found the old picture of my mother on one of the shelves in the studio. It had hung in my father's house for years. One day I came and instead of the picture there was a pale empty mark on the wall. I didn't ask and he didn't say and both of us knew what the pale empty mark was, and the next day his second wife moved into the house. Later they painted the wall and the pale empty mark disappeared, and later, when I came one day to visit my father he handed me a parcel wrapped up and tied with string. I didn't ask and he didn't say and we both knew what was inside the parcel, which to tell the truth I never opened and left wrapped up on the studio shelf. Sometimes we went to the cemetery, my sisters and I. He never went. Afterward we stopped going too. The thorns grew wild. The stone sank. Ten years passed. Twenty years passed. The thorns must have covered the stone, which was low anyway and must be on a level with the ground by now.

Thirty years later, that evening when I sat next to him, his face was crumpled and he cried all the time.

I have to talk to you, he said and cried all the time.

So let's talk, I said.

Let's go into the little room, he said.

Right, let's go into the little room, I said.

His clear, blue eyes were frozen and he cried all the time.

I don't know what to do, he said.

What about, I asked.

I don't know where to be buried, he said.

But father, I said.

He cried all the time.

I don't know where to be buried, he said and cried.

His eyes glittered now, motionless, two blue stones.

He said: They say there's an empty plot next to Batya.

Batya was his second wife. It was the day after the funeral.

Buy the empty plot, I said.

I can't, he said.

Why, I said.

I can't do it to your mother, he said. I can't prefer one woman to the other.

But father, I said.

His face suddenly turned grey.

No, he said. I'll be buried alone. I can't prefer one woman to the other.

It was hard for me to look at him. I thought that he hadn't spoken about her for thirty years.

He said: They say that I should do whatever makes me feel better. That I should be buried wherever I feel better.

It was hard for me to look at him. His chin trembled slightly.

What do they know, he said.

Yes, I said.

His face was still grey, the color of wood, and only his eyes shone like two headlamps on a wooden box.

I'll be buried alone, he repeated. I can't prefer one woman to the other.

I reminded him that he had lived with Batya for thirty years. He said: What are thirty years.

His teeth chattered. He said: I missed her for thirty years.

His voice was now strange, grating, and he gripped the fingers of one hand in the other like iron pliers.

Yes, I'd better be buried alone, he bit off shortly.

His teeth were still chattering and he pushed both hands into his mouth and sat like that for a long time, his mouth muzzled, black as a vice.

It was hard for me to look at him. His face was covered with his bitten nails. I thought, my father, an old man, is chewing bitten nails. I thought that he hadn't spoken about her for thirty years. His nails were hard, cut, and I thought about the chalk, about the materials of the blood and the materials of the earth. I thought about how he would come and sit in silence, oh my father, how he sat in silence, and I said to myself that there is a spirit in man, a spirit in man, my father.

I said to myself, most wonderful. His face was grey, tired. He coughed, his throat was hoarse with crying. When he woke up his eyes blazed outside his face. They were cold and there was a mineral power in them.

Yes, I'll be buried alone, he repeated resolutely. His coughing grew worse and he got up and stood in the middle of the room, swaying as if he were hanging in the air. I'll be buried alone, he repeated swaying in the middle of the room. He looked for a wall.

A few months later I heard him climbing up the wooden stairs panting hard. He was very pale when he came in.

I went to ask, he said.

I asked, what.

His eyes looked at me, dry, extinguished.

Yes, I went to ask, he said. He smiled miserably.

The plot's still vacant, he said.

Buy it, I said.

I can't, he said.

Buy it, I said.

I made coffee. We did not speak for a long time. He said: It's a difficult decision. His hand shook. He said: I can't be alone in the ground. The coffee spilt on his trousers and he put the cup down on the table and carefully cleaned his trousers.

His voice was passionate. No, I can't be alone in the ground, he repeated. His hands were still shaking and he went on drinking slowly holding the cup in both hands.

A few days later my sister found him crumpled like a cushion dead on the floor.

The vacant plot was registered in his name.

They said we should make twin gravestones and write the same text on the stone. One of them even said that he would probably feel better if there was a similar text on the gravestone.

When I moved out of the Haifa apartment this week I found my mother's picture on the shelf in the studio, still wrapped in the same paper and tied with the same string. I took it with me to Tel Aviv and opened the parcel.

My mother looked out, very young.

I cleaned the glass, stuck a nail in the wall, and hung it low, close to the floor. Since the door is always open she only peeps out sideways. Every day she looks younger.

My father died in December. It was raining hard. We didn't go this year.

Translated by Dalya Bilu

N obody on the street could believe he'd sold his magnificent stamp collection. They said he must have bought land, houses, shops, diamonds. There were stamps worth four carats, they said. Maybe five, they said. Afterwards, when his only daughter, Ruthie, whom he called Rutchen, disappear :d, they said that with one stamp she could have taken a trip around the world; and when she came back, her eyes white and her skin green—it seemed a little strange to come back like this, with white eyes and green skin, after a trip around the world—they said maybe it was disappointment in love, maybe she went looking for a husband and didn't find one, maybe a trip around the world wasn't such a big deal. He welcomed her with a growl and Mrs. Klein, who saw her come home, said she went in without a purse, without a suitcase, her coat over her shoulders, and she suddenly seemed shorter in the shoulders, as if her shoulders had caved in. As it happened, I saw her too, hunched, wrapped up like a parcel, holding her raincoat with both hands, as if she were naked under the coat, dragging lopsidedly along the street in the wind and standing outside the house for a long time, leaning on the stone fence without going up. And then she pushed herself forward as violently as if she were pushing a freight car.

And then we heard the growling and it was clear that they weren't expecting her, that they didn't know. Afterwards we kept on hearing it from our window night after night—long, strange, unending, like a moan, or like the sound of his bus in the morning when it wouldn't start. We couldn't hear what he said, only Gerda's silences moving back and forth in the window all the time, while he hardly stood up, just sat there bent over with his chin on his belly and the growl coming out of his belly.

As for the true story, it broke into the street in small, low waves, accompanied by little laughs from Mrs. Borak and Mrs. Klein and Mr. "Everything Cheap" and the rest of the neighbors. By then the growling had already stopped, and Gerda—a sticklike woman who stood for years leaning against the door, until she became part of the door itself—now sat at the table for hours, picking at the little pink flowers on the oilcloth. He said that soon there would be nothing left to pick at, and what she would pick at would be her fingers. Yeah, my fingers, my fingers, she yelled.

And then came the evening when all the lights suddenly went out and only her scream rose from the dark house: Small change doesn't burn, doesn't tear, what burns is a human being. That's what Mrs. Borak said, but Mrs. Klein said she screamed that it was all because of the small change, all because of the small change. To tell the truth, I was at home then and what I heard was a kind of dry crackle spilling into the darkness, and when I went to the window he was standing there, on the balcony, in the dark, grunting like an empty barrel.

Have you ever seen an owl's eyes? said Rutchen. He was cursing, that was a curse. You couldn't even make out his body in the dark, only his voice and his eyes, as if his voice were coming from his eyes. She smiled a pale smile. Have you ever felt as if someone's voice was coming out of his eyes? she smiled again a pale smile. And do you know what he said? she said. He said small change is like a human being, you have to bury it, he said, you can only finish with it in the ground. The pale smile spread over her whole face, making it suddenly look small. His eyes never moved, she said, and in the night they were white, you understand? She looked at me with her head thrown back, her hand moved up to her throat. Her face took on a stubborn look, as if trying to understand but not coming anywhere near understanding. Of course you can't burn small change, she said.

This was already after everything and after the funeral, and Gerda was already sitting on the balcony in the evening again, picking at the green oilcloth, her face the color of roasted coffee. We sat on a bench in the park at the end of the street. It was a nice evening. There were hardly any people in the park, and it was quiet, with the slow pulsing of the revolving sprinklers and the water spreading in big, expanding circles. She said: It was like him, what drove me mad was the small change. I told her that for years we had watched every night. She didn't even smile. What can you see from the window, you can't see it from the window, she said. I said that for years we had watched him wrapping the stacks and sorting. Oh, she said, that's nothing, not even the beginning. She spoke slowly. There was fear in her voice.

Yes, I said, we would watch him from the kitchen window wrapping the small change in tinfoil. Every night we saw the little columns wrapped in tinfoil.

Oh, the towers, she said, there were towers of fives, towers of tens, towers of ones. He said it wasn't the size that counted or the amount, what counted was something else, and that's what he said about the stamps, too, and about life, too, really. She suddenly drew in her head and her face was suffused with dark spots like inkspots. They looked transparent, spreading into her skin like ink into paper.

She looked at me for a long time.

It's not what you think, she said.

I didn't say anything. I didn't know what she meant. She looked at me for a long time again and laughed a quiet, violent laugh that made the inkspots under her skin grow bigger. That's where I first saw the monster, she said. Her words sounded familiar and I said that everyone had a little monster in some window or other. She laughed quietly, violently, not listening. The truth is, it was there long before that, the monster was there long before that, she said and looked at me for a long time, as if looking through me at some empty, unidentified place behind the bench. I said there wasn't any monster in the window. And then I said that he was simply counting small change. When he met me in the street he said so. He said that in the morning a man needs small change.

Her laughter expanded now, making the inkspots under her skin grow even bigger.

Yes, she said, in the morning a man needs small change, every day he said that to me, when I was still a little girl he said that to me, he said that the most expensive stamp in the world was a penny stamp.

Her face turned purple, cross-hatched like a rash of thorns. She was silent for a moment, then she laughed dryly. He couldn't have guessed, she said, he couldn't have guessed that it coiled like a snake, that it glittered all the time, it moved all the time, he couldn't have guessed, he thought that all at once the riddle had been solved.

I didn't ask which riddle.

And that's what killed him, she said. Her voice sounded depressed. You think it was my revenge, oh no, but then what was it? You think I know what it was? The depression in her voice increased. Look at the trees, she said.

I looked at the trees. There was a magnificent light on the trees on the slope, wrapping them in ribbons of radiance that broke up into a thousand coins of silver and gold, cascading in long trains down the tree trunks and the mountain, and all at once the mountain turned into a moving heap of coins, the ground and the trees and the walls of the houses and the roofs and the car bodies and the high greenness of the treetops further down along the line of the boulevard. Everything gleamed. Everything moved. Everything came apart in one mad rush as if it was spilling out of some huge basket, and in the radiant, dazzling light all you could see were the holes of the net from which this hail of coins was pouring, a hail of silver and gold that became a molten surface, turning the mountain into a steep wall of coins, a gleaming dancing wall of faces and branches and masks and letters. It lasted a moment. Maybe an hour. The wall swayed. The mountain shook. Above the mountain, the horizon line was sharp, rigid, petrified, and the sky was narrow, alien, compressed into a long rectangle, into a closed box, and for a moment I nearly panicked, for a moment I said to myself that I too had caught the disease. The sky looked closed, stood apart from the celebration. But the mountain was still full of coins, everything was still rushing down, everything merged, everything ran together, gleamed in wildly scribbled lines and crooked contours, everything flew. And then suddenly the gold turned to brass, the silver to lead, and the huge leaden coins came pelting down on the mountainside as at the beginning of winter, as in a terrible storm.

You see? said Rutchen. She sounded excited. You see? she said.

It seemed to me that I understood what she meant. It seemed to me that the light waves were turning into sound waves, and I said to myself: Look, look, I've caught the disease. It seemed to me that some mechanism had broken down into vague elements, everything that belonged to earth, fire, air and water, that belonged to thoughts and fears, and I said to myself: The mountain's full of coins, Rutchen. Oh Rutchen, how quickly the gold turns to lead, how quickly it turns to zinc. I said to myself: Of course, I saw the hail, the faces, the people, the tree trunks, the gold scales on the tree trunks, the snakes, the old letters, the old kings, suddenly I remembered her, a little girl, walking round the rooms opposite us, saying short nervous words, words without endings, swallowing the ends of words. I remembered: To go to another country, to go to another country. I remembered: And I was left naked and bare. I wanted to tell her that you couldn't just pack up your things, that it was a bad idea. But it was quiet now. The light calmed down. The radiation began to shrink, became infrared. Among the trees there were only a few matches burning now, and afterwards floating on top of the mountain a small dark copper stain turned blood red.

Terrible, she said.

Her face was swollen and you could feel the slow burning blush of shame.

Yes, he loved it, she said, to see how it shone, to see it in piles, he arranged it in piles, the whole house was full of piles, he called them towers, maybe they really were towers.

I didn't ask towers of what.

That's what I understood before I left, she said.

I looked at her leaning against the arm of the bench. Now too I didn't ask what. The light was going down, falling on the roots of the tree, making them glow at the bottom of the trunks, at the meeting point with the earth. It was hard to tell which way the wind was coming from, if it was blowing from the mountain or the sea, but you could clearly see how it was shaking the trunks right down to the bottom, shaking the grass and the tops of the bushes and the leaves and the black tunnels between the bushes with a loud commotion. But we were alone there in the park. That's what I understood before I left, she repeated. She asked if I knew the story about the cat. I said that I hadn't known the cat. She said: And he blamed mother, he said she loved the cat too much, that's why the cat took liberties and that's what happened in the end. It jumped onto my stamps, he said.

I asked what kind of stamps he had collected.

She said he had collected stamps with faces, with birds of prey, and antisemitic stamps. Later on he exchanged the faces for birds of prey. Later on he exchanged the birds of prey too and he was left with only the antisemitic stamps. He had the biggest collection of antisemitic stamps.

I asked what antisemitic stamps were.

He had rare ones, she said.

I asked for an example.

She said he had a postcard with a stamp of a Nazi horse stamping on the globe and she remembered the date, he looked at the date every day, it was on the nineteenth of October 1942, and there was a postmark without an address, *Europische Post Kongress,* and he said, that was before you were born, Rutchen, but it will go on to the end of the world, it will go on as long as there are people in the world.

She was speaking fast.

Those were his words, you understand? Then she said that he had a copper-colored stamp of Hitler with the postmark April 20, 1944, *Grossdeutsche Reich General Gouvernment,* and a stamp with Stalin's head, a beautiful green-black stamp, Stalin's head in the middle and on the right the English crown, on the left the hammer and sickle, and 1939 written on top of the English crown, 1944 on top of the hammer and sickle, and at the bottom it said: *This is a Jewish war.*

She was still speaking fast.

This is a Jewish war, get it? Then she said that he had a bright red stamp, really blazing red, also with Stalin on the left and the King of England on the right, and he looked at this stamp too every day, he turned that page every day, he couldn't go to sleep without looking at that page, she said. Then she added that she always looked at his hands when he was holding this page, she didn't know why she did it, but that's what she did.

She was still speaking fast.

After he sat with this stamp he closed the album and put it in the cupboard. And then he began preparing the small change.

Suddenly her eyes filled with tears.

It's just incredible, she said.

I asked what other stamps he had.

Antisemitic ones you mean, she said gleefully. She said he had a stamp issued by Khomeini in honor of Sadat's assassin, and the Egyptians quickly bought up all the stamps from all the collections in the world, the whole series, so that there wasn't one stamp like it in the world, and then he decided that he had to have one, and he searched for a whole year long, and after a year he found one in Canada, in Montreal and he bought it from Montreal, a black-and-white stamp, the murderer in a white robe in a window of black sky, laughing inside the black sky, and when he got that stamp he said again that it's a story without an end, it never ends, and he began talking about the English penny stamp again, the most expensive stamp in the world worth three million dollars, a penny stamp.

She rubbed her forehead, making signs as if to a deaf-mute, pressing against the back of the bench. That's it, she said, and then he sold them, he traded them for small change.

All at once her face turned white, fixing me with a glittering, violet eye, and now I clearly saw him sitting on the balcony, half naked, hairy as an animal; I remembered his strong, tyrannical hands, the wine color of his eyes, the little squares with swift horses in the wind, winged horses, naked archers shooting at the sun and birds choked by snakes, and I remembered him, a short man with a rounded head sitting all summer, every summer, bent over the bright pages as if sharing in some hidden secret, as if drawing closer to the pulse of the world, and by then the formica table had long ago been transformed into extraterritorial ground, long ago become an island in international waters, and he, as keeper of the seal, cataloging, sticking, removing, transferring, sometimes peering up close without moving, sometimes slapping his knees in excitement, and it gave off a sweet smell, said Rutchen, it gave off a faraway smell, the page looked like a big map of the sky, and bent over, without raising his head, without a word— sometimes arranging the pages by subject and sometimes by place, sometimes according to generations that suddenly seemed shortlived, the continents shrunken, Cuba next to Mecca, Titus's arch next to the black stone, and you could find Genghis Khan next to Jesus, Napoleon next to Cyrus the Great, and it gave off a sweet smell, said Rutchen, it gave off a faraway smell, and what was fascinating were the teeth and the corners, she said.

I looked at her. She too had short clumsy hands and the same wine-colored eyes, and I suddenly felt a kind of compassion. She looked at me. Her face said something about the wolf never changing his ways, and that was what I thought all the time she looked at me. She said that Gerda thought they should keep them in a safe, it was enough to steal one stamp, she said, but he said that stamps were like bread, you have to have them on the table every day.

Suddenly she looked at me suspiciously. What were you just thinking of? she said. Her eyes were on me, empty, very close, and I told her I had just remembered the story about how some people were buying a plot of land from an Indian and he asked them, how high and how deep are you buying? She smiled painfully. I told her that the Indians wrote the word Earth with a capital letter. She stared at me with dark eyes and smiled painfully again, and I told her that I had once met an Indian in Arizona next to the big crater, near the red cave city, and he was naked and he was red, and instead of a fig leaf he had marvelous blue turquoises hanging between his legs, strings of marvelous little blue rocks instead of a fig leaf, and he told me the story, Earth with a capital letter, he said.

She didn't take her red, swollen eyes off me. A strange smile, more like a grimace, crossed her face. That's it, she said as if she were saying something terrible.

He was a bus driver. Since he always worked the morning shift he got his small change ready every evening. First thing in the morning, he said, a man needs small change. No one was surprised that he always worked the morning shift, and for years, at four o'clock in the morning, we heard him turning on the light in the stairwell. Then we heard him go downstairs. And then we heard footsteps in the empty street and the bus engine groaning, and then came the silence, and we knew that Mr. Shlezi had driven off. Sometimes, in the summer, when the windows were open, we also heard the bread popping out of the toaster. He always wore sunglasses, even in winter, in the rain, and I sometimes saw him trudging down the street in the rain, short, small, the two round black spots dripping on his face, walking holding his hands on his stomach, his broad hands putting a strange kind of pressure on his stomach, or suddenly stretching his body, swelling, and making a dash for the huge waiting machine. He liked distances without horizons, said Rutchen, he liked to see up close, what was happening on the road up close, the telegraph pole was far enough, drivers who looked too far ahead were accident prone, he said, and to tell the truth in forty years he never had an accident. Like in the New Testament, the innocent had to die guilty, he said, that was what happened on the road, the innocent died guilty on the road.

But the bus no longer stood in the street then, and it was already after he had sold the stamp collection and the whole house was filled with small change in little stacks wrapped in tracing paper and thin tinfoil, in all the cupboards and all the tables and all the drawers and in the kitchen too. It was in boxes and in suitcases, and by then he wasn't doing anything, only transferring the stacks, smoothing the paper and turning it over, and then closing and folding, and then pressing it down. He smoothed the paper and pressed it down on every stack, and then he wrote it down. He had a special notebook where he wrote everything down. The size, and the amount, and he never counted, said Rutchen, he knew with his eyes without counting, he could see in the dark and he knew, and nobody was allowed to come near, she said, mother never went near, and they didn't talk about it, she said, they didn't ask, mother never asked, she only looked, and gradually her face swelled up, gradually her eyes grew small and she turned blue, she said she had ants in her fingers, afterwards she said it was the rustling of the paper that had got into her fingers, and at night they really did swell up, she said, and they looked exactly like the stacks, round, swollen, with transparent skin the color of silver, but he said that there was nothing to be afraid of and it was shut up in the cupboards, it was all shut up in the cupboards, he said.

The idea came to her by chance, of course. By chance she heard in the street that the Israeli lira was the size of a two-franc piece, and in Zurich there were automats that turned two francs into small change. There were some Israelis, they said, who put liras into the automats and got out two francs in small change. It looked good. It was after the currency was changed, but she was sure he hadn't thrown out the liras, she was sure even before she went looking. And then she went home and looked into the cupboards. And after that in the linen boxes under the beds. And in the chest. And behind the books. And in the vases. There were rolls of half-shekels. Of shekels. But in the end she found the liras. She identified them without opening the paper. There was nothing simpler, she said.

On the first day it worked perfectly. She did it in the automat of a giant department store. The store was crowded. There were people rushing around her all the time, there was no waiting line for the automat. The people rushing around apparently didn't need small change, and in the evening she strolled along Lake Geneva and ate a fat sausage with mustard. Afterwards she sat in a café on the lakeside and licked a huge helping of ice cream. And then she went right down to the bank of the lake and sat. It was a silvery night. It was already quite late. Swans floated on the water, illuminated in the transparent silver light. They had no heads or necks, only bodies moving in the water, floating quietly in a quiet movement, like shining black coats moving over the waves. Their silky feathers gleamed, their heads so enfolded in their bodies that they looked the wrong way round, floating in the direction opposite to their bodies. The man sitting next to her said: There's nothing to be afraid of, they fold their heads into their bodies to go to sleep. He was sitting with a box of pears and she gave him a bit of small change and he gave her a few long slender pears dripping with golden juice, and she sat and looked at the headless swans and ate the golden pears, and the next day she went back to the automat and the next day too there was a lot of traffic and people dragging boxes of merchandise from the storeroom and back again, but she inserted a lira into the slot and pressed and then she inserted another lira and pressed again and then she inserted another lira and pressed again, and in the end her hand was full and sweating slightly and she put the money in her purse, but her hand, empty now, was still sweating. The purse suddenly felt a little heavy on her shoulder, dragging her shoulder down, but she inserted a lira into the slot and pressed and instead of a faded old lira, her palm was full of small change again, pretty shining Swiss money, really pretty, only her palm was a little sweaty and she thought that perhaps she should stop, perhaps she was a little tired and she would go and buy herself something to drink. She opened her purse and put a little scent on her sweaty palm and emerged from the corner where the automat was, and two women came walking very quietly on either side of her, coming very quietly closer to her body until she almost felt their bodies pressing against her on either side and she said excuse me I'm in a hurry and they squeezed her body a little and said please come with us and pushed her slightly forward, very slight pushes close to the walls which were painted a quiet pale green color and the air in the long quiet corridor was warm and pleasant and there was pleasant music playing and she wanted to ask where they were going, what they wanted, but she didn't ask, urged forward by the slight pushes of the very quiet women who didn't say a word and pushed her slowly with little movements of their elbows into a side room at the end of the corridor. A nicely furnished room, which was also painted a quiet pale green color with an executive desk and an executive chair with a lightly rocking man on it whose head turned in all directions as if he was a strange gigantic doll and the two women said please sit down. But they didn't wait for her to sit and they sat her down with little movements of their elbows, with the same light imperceptible pressure on a pale green leather chair, and remained standing very quietly on either side of the chair, leaning on her lightly, on her body, and isolated voices were heard here and there in the long corridor and the sound of pleasant music reached her ears.

It was very pleasant music, she said.

There was a pause. I waited for her to go on but she was silent, staring right into my face. Her voice was pale, monotonous, as after years of silence, the sentences more and more unfinished, more and more erratic, more and more absurd, and it was impossible to tell if her story was about to end or had just begun. Her face, which was white, looked thin now, and she held her head pressed hard against the bench, elongated, thrust rigidly backward, like a person standing with his back to the wall.

After all, she said in a loud, sudden voice, without continuing.

Now too there was silence. I didn't ask her after all what. She said: And then I remembered the packets in the hotel, the stacks rolled up in silver foil with a twist at the top, the way he did it.

The corners of her lips rose as if to smile, but instead of smiling they twisted into an ugly grimace, stubbornly examining my face. Her own grew sharp and venomous.

Suddenly I understood, she said.

She looked at me again, still examining my face.

I mean I thought I did, she said. Her speech was still sudden, abrupt, as if a petrified stratum of memories had suddenly been jolted.

Now too there was silence. The two of us were alone in the park. Lines of fire were still running over the lawn, down where the air had reddened on the snakeskin at the bottom of the tree trunks. Then a wind blew up, tossing among the dark bushes. There was a strong smell of grass and wilted blossoms, a smell of cut-down trees and gouged trunks, of rotting roots. Then the air turned into smoke creeping over the ground. The backs of the benches were the color of marble and behind every bench stood a barrel of dynamite. Rutchen did not take her eyes off me, examined me suspiciously. Her pupils dilated with a solemn light, the kind of light where everything suddenly splits open, the world splits open, is torn apart inside, lit low down like a low fire, full of patches and ropes and pieces of iron, and in every voice a mighty orchestra sounds. Suddenly I remembered how in Nesher, in the factory, I once brought a huge thermos to my uncle, my father's sister's husband, on the night shift. It was a hot night, and he was standing in the furnace room, covered with dust, leaning on the iron bar attached to the furnace, barefoot in the heaps of iron, his curly black head a pile of dust and his face too, slowly opening the thermos and slowly gulping down the cold lemonade and explaining something about life to me between gulps, and that life is like an iron bar, at first the bar gets hot but it doesn't glow, its rays are infrared. When the temperature rises it begins to glow, at first the glow's dark red, then light red, then yellow, then it turns white-hot, and after the white comes the blue, the violet comes at the end. What comes after the violet is invisible, it's like the stars, he said, red stars are cold, and I'm an electrician, he said, I'll die of an electric shock. He died of an electric shock.

I told her. She asked me why I had told her. I said I didn't know. She studied me suspiciously again.

Naturally, she said. She asked what his name was.

I told her.

She asked what he was like.

Nice, I said.

So was papa, really, she said. She asked me if I knew his name.

I said no.

She gave me a shocked look.

Naturally, she said again. Then she asked me what we called him.

Shlezi, I said.

She said: That's a pet name you know.

I said that we were fond of him.

She gave me a shocked look again. Ma never called him by his name, she said.

I didn't ask what she called him.

Can you understand that? she said. Her eyes, which looked tired, suddenly filled with blood, as if there were nothing left there but a scar, like a brand, and after a minute she went on with her story, speaking at the same rhythm as before, as if she had never stopped. The man on the executive chair asked her where she was from. She said from Israel. He said he knew. She felt she had said something wrong. Close to her, very close, on the chair revolving next to her, rocked a woman whose face was in different places all the time, and someone from somewhere at the side said: *Ja, aus Israel.* The woman on the swivel chair, whose face kept revolving in the air, sniggered *Ja, aus Israel,* and then she sniggered again, and her snigger grew smaller and smaller, narrower and narrower, the wider the revolutions on the giddy chair. The man whose voice was coming from somewhere on the side said: *Ja, immer aus Israel, das wissen wir schon,* and the woman on the revolving chair sniggered an even smaller and narrower snigger, revolving on the chair in the same monotonous and merciless rhythm that slightly twisted her lips, and Rutchen kept watching her lips. She said to herself: She has dark narrow lips, dead lips, that was what she kept saying to herself over and over: She has dark narrow lips, dead lips, and from the crowded department store came the sound of doors opening and pleasant music. She tried to reconstruct what had happened but she was

absolutely unable to reconstruct what had happened. There was a
sound of movement from the executive chair facing her and she said to
herself: He's talking to me, he's asking me something, but she heard
only the sound of the doors opening and the pleasant music, she felt
the soothing pale green of the walls touching her skin, the quiet steady
vicious hatred and a kind of absolute emptiness inside her body, inside
the deep memory of her body, but opposite her on the chair the revolving head kept on with the *immer aus Israel,* and she heard her own
voice asking how long it would take. The man's voice coming from
somewhere on the side said: That we don't know. Next to her, close to
her, very close to her, in the air next to her, the woman's head revolved,
decapitated, floating in the air above the soothing pale green of the
chair and the soothing pale green of the walls and the absolute emptiness inside her body inside the deep memory of her body, and still it
was all just a bad joke but already she heard her own voice in a low terrified shriek: How long? She shrieked in terror, and close to her even
closer to her pressing even closer to her body the woman's decapitated
head went on revolving on the chair in the same slow monotonous
merciless rhythm and the man's voice coming from somewhere on the
side said: That we don't know, the decapitated head was revolving
right in front of her now and terrified she shrieked again: But how
long? The man on the executive chair repeated with his quiet smile:
That we don't know, and by now she couldn't see him either only his
face floating detached over the chair as if in a horror movie and the
quiet steady vicious hatred the absolute emptiness inside her body inside the deep memory of her body, and she had no time to think yet
but time enough to feel the fear, light and weightless, sinking inside
her body.

They asked for her purse. She put it on the table. A moment passed.
The man waited. Then he opened it. Then he turned it upside down
on the table and the small change piled up on the table, gleaming
Swiss coins, coins of ten and coins of twenty. He counted them in silence. He asked if that was all. She said that was all. He asked for her
shoulder bag. She gave him her shoulder bag. Her hands shook. A
sound stirred on the chair opposite and she sensed her hands shaking
and the man on the chair looking not inside the bag but at her shaking
hands. She looked at her hands too. They looked big, they looked
bigger every minute, shaking as if they had Parkinson's, like her father's
father shook with Parkinson's and they couldn't stop the shaking till he

died. She saw him lying on the floor shaking after he died. She saw it clearly now. Suddenly her hands looked to her like his hands. She remembered his hands as if they were alive. She remembered them shaking alive on his corpse. Suddenly a terrible idea struck her, it struck her forehead and pierced her skull and came out the other side like a savage drill boring into her head deep down inside her skull. She couldn't stop shaking.

The man held the shoulder bag and looked at her hands.

Ja, he said and overturned the bag.

First the folding umbrella fell out. The little make-up bag. The red comb. The packet of colored pencils she had bought there that day. The round green mirror. And then there was a clattering sound and a pile of one lira coins fell out.

The man in the chair opposite her didn't move. He raised his eyes. Then he dropped his eyes. Then he put the coins down one by one on the table and counted aloud. There were twenty-one. He asked if that was all. She said that was all. He asked what she was doing with them. She said her father collected coins. He asked why her father collected coins. She said she didn't know. He looked at her. He waited.

That I don't know, she said, sitting without moving, the Parkinson's hands on her knees. She lifted them into the air, so that they wouldn't be stuck to her knees, but they went on shaking in the air, alien, big, almost gigantic, detached from her body, immense uncontrollable hands, like two long swollen stuffed hands hanging there on her body. She tried to stop the shaking, which only increased the wild twitching. Suddenly she remembered inserting a coin into the slot and then the click. And again a coin and again the click. And the metallic chill on her palm and the sweat.

The man on the executive chair kept his eyes on her Parkinson's hands all the time. He asked again why her father had collected coins.

He said that a man needs small change, she said.

She didn't know how she said it. She felt as if a horse had kicked her when she said it.

Natürlich, said the man on the chair.

He spoke to me without turning his head in my direction and he was very quiet all the time, he didn't look at me to hear what I said, and I didn't hear what he said only his voice and afterwards a different voice in the opposite direction of his voice, and when I turned round the voice stopped talking, and the hunt began.

And maybe I didn't turn round, she said.

Suddenly she fell silent.

My head aches, she said.

I said maybe we shouldn't talk about it.

She looked at me in astonishment.

What? she said.

I said maybe tomorrow.

Oh no, she said, pressing her eyelids as if she had only just realized that there was a terrible pain there. Her eyelids were inflamed. The things I dream, she said. I said everybody dreams. She said: And the places I go. I said everybody does, everybody, the sense of falling, the giddiness, the monstrous roads, and I said that everything runs in steep tunnels, hangs from cliffs, and the birds of prey. She said: What do you mean, the birds of prey? I said that last night, for example, I dreamt there was a bird of prey on the lintel of our door behind the wall. I saw it clearly coming out of the wall and I wanted to scream: There's a bird of prey in the house, there's a bird of prey in the house, and then the wall closed up.

She looked at me in astonishment.

Last night? she said. She asked if I'd read about it. I said that once I read that contrary to what most people thought they didn't fly swiftly when hunting their prey, the hunting was done in slow flight, and I told her that I'd read that the most impressive hunting method was the one where the prey was caught in mid-flight, in the middle of the sky, in this hunting method the prey was totally exposed, it had no place to hide and nowhere to escape to. The hawk, for example, I read was good at pursuing birds in open spaces and it fed on songbirds, so it was very active early in the morning, because that was when songbirds were found.

She looked at me in excitement. Songbirds? she said. There was passionate desire in her voice. She asked about the speed. I said: Three hundred miles an hour. The gold eagle, for example, dived on its prey at a speed of three hundred miles an hour. She asked about the vulture. I said that the vulture, which fed on carrion, circled its prey like a huge butterfly. It advanced in hops with its shoulder feathers bristling and its wings spread as its thick beak prepared to tear the skin.

She was still looking at me passionately. You've forgotten that papa collected stamps with birds of prey, she said in excitement, stealthily wiping her eyes, and then pressing her eyelids hard, examining me to see if I was listening. He had a wonderful collection of birds of prey, she said. Her white face was now illuminated by the light from the lamp that had gone on behind the bench—thin, childish, very like the face I had seen for years in the gold light of the room facing our window. And for a moment the years were wiped out, the dramas, catastrophes, screams and fear, the lost albums, and all that was left was a little girl sitting alone in a room illuminated by lamplight, asking about birds of prey, staring at me and saying: Songbirds? Songbirds? Lifting her little girl's face, looking out of the window. And the courtyard was swarming with pimps, prostitutes, respectable lawyers, respectable businessmen, swarming with cats and dogs, shoe-shop owners and furniture-shop owners, groaning, coming, going, buttoning, unbuttoning, and I wanted to say to her: yes, at a speed of three hundred miles an hour, Rutchen, a speed of three hundred miles an hour. I wanted to say to her: Vultures, Rutchen, because of the wind, are attached to mountainous regions, and they have very keen sight, eagle-eyes, they can locate carrion thirteen miles away, from thirteen miles away their eyes can trap a dead bird.

They were waiting for Herr Zutter. It took time. The man in the armchair laughed contemptuously. He said: How slow the machine of justice is. The woman on the chair laughed too. Just then Herr Zutter came. His eyes were alert and he looked straight at the table. Her shoulder bag was lying there, open and empty, and the money was in a neat pile. He asked something. She repeated that her father said a man needs small change; in the morning, he said, in the morning a man needs small change. Herr Zutter sniggered. Then he said that she must be careful, she should be careful because from now on everything would be written down. She didn't answer. He waited a minute. She didn't answer. Her feet were sweating in her shoes, but she sat still, frozen, without moving. It seemed to her that she heard the sound of footsteps dragging slowly in the corridor, but nobody in the room said anything and nobody moved and only the quiet soothing pale green walls began turning round and round as if powered by a machine. She felt she had to stop the machine, but the heads on the chairs were also turning round and round, her own gigantic hands, the backs of the chairs, the curtains, the ashtrays, the comb on the desk, the pile of coins, and other hands in other corners of the room, other walls behind the chairs. She pressed her hands hard against her knees. Anyway,

anyway, she said. She said it in Hebrew, frightened because she said it in Hebrew, and suddenly the walls stopped turning, the emptiness in her body gripped like a vice, the pale green color quieted down, the man in the armchair opposite turned up the volume of the radio, smoking, and she felt the light touch of terror, sitting as if in a dream, sliding silently and surely into the abyss. And then she heard Herr Zutter. He said she should hurry up, it was late and it was a long drive, and she really should hurry up.

It was raining, she said, but my throat was full of dry crystals like beads of hail.

And we drove in the police car, behind an iron grill, she said, and it really was a long drive. When they stopped she got out. There was a high house. They told her to go inside and hurry up. Everything happened in a hurry. She hurried up. There were long corridors with doors and more corridors with doors. The corridors were empty and you could hardly see the walls only the doors and they opened a door and led her in. Herr Zutter asked for the bag. She gave him the bag. He told her to get undressed. Then he told her to wait. Then took the bag and went out and locked the door. There was a chair there and she got undressed and sat down on the chair. Time passed. The room was empty. The cold of the chair burned her skin and she sat and looked at her body as if at some strange animal.

Time passed. She went up to the door. The door was locked and she went back to the chair. Again time passed. Her hands stopped shaking. Now they were small, unnaturally small, almost like a child's hands. She felt a terrible shame, sitting in the empty room, on the chair, looking at her own body, feeling something, she didn't know what, turning into a concrete, meaningless thing. Her father appeared in a flash. She heard him say: The disgrace, she saw him from the depths of her back. Oh no, it's different, she said. Her skin prickled. Time passed. Again time passed. She felt her body becoming hollow, felt his weakness and wildness and idiocy in her blood. Everything whirled in crazy vertigo, the stupidity that had led her astray, and the disgrace, from here it would begin again, the disgrace, humiliated, the terror that made her jump, the hand gripping her shoulder—it was the policewoman who made her stand up and felt her all over her body, felt her skin, in every corner, all over her skin, as if she had coins hidden under her skin. Then she ran her hands over her once again, groping, and turned around without a word and went out of the room and after that another policewoman came in and told her to get dressed and take off her watch and her rings and earrings, and she took them off and put them in a heap on the chair but the policewoman said: The watch, the watch too, and she took off her watch but the policewoman said: And the little ring too, and she pulled the little ring but it wouldn't come off and she said: I've had it since I was a little girl, but the policewoman said: Everything, everything, everything left on the body, and she brought soap and rubbed, and then Herr Zutter came and said they were leaving and they got into the armored car again behind the iron grill again in the rainy streets in the evening coming down on the beautiful bustling city and the gleaming lights in the grand shops and cafés, and she said: Everything's open, it's still early, and Herr Zutter said: Yes, we have to be there before four because the examining magistrate leaves at four, and she said: I haven't got a watch, they took my watch away. He didn't answer. The rain hit the roof of the car. She asked where she was. He didn't answer. She asked where they were taking her. He didn't answer. And she said: Oh God it's not rain it's a storm it can't be anything but a storm and would Herr Zutter please turn round just once. He didn't turn round even once.

What shall I do, she said.

He didn't turn his head.

Sign a confession. Here in Switzerland, you have nothing to fear. When someone confesses and repents we let him go.

She said she was afraid.

He said: Here in Switzerland you have nothing to fear. This is a free country. What we hate is a lie. Nobody in Switzerland has ever been punished for the truth. What we can't forgive is a lie.

She shivered.

What our judges hate is a lie.

She shivered.

He said: If you tell lies you'll rot in jail. For the truth we send people home here, understand?

I remember his back, she said, he didn't turn his head, what I remember is his back. He had a brown leather jacket on and I remember his voice coming out of the leather jacket. That's what I advise you to do, he said. He had a soft voice, actually, a woolly voice. It seemed to me that his leather jacket was made of wool.

You should know that the law is always right, he said and smiled, looking at her now obliquely, a look that spread like threads over her body, sticking to her like a spider and tightening in threads around her body.

Have you ever seen the way a spider works? That was how his eyes worked, she said. And then the fear came back to her, pressing on her throat.

I hope you haven't got any more on your body, he said. And then he said he hoped she didn't have any more in the hotel. She said she didn't. He didn't ask the name of the hotel, only his eyes spreading round her body, and then the crazy idea came to her, then she asked if they had already passed the square where the gold was buried. He asked what gold. She said: The Paraden Platz, where the safes were, her grandfather had one too. He asked where her grandfather was. She didn't answer. He said he was sorry, Switzerland only looked after the gold. He asked what the connection was. She said there wasn't one. He laughed a little. And it's impossible to open of course, that's the code, the secret, he said. Again he laughed a little. You have to understand, the whole world understands, he said. He turned round slowly to face her. And you stole from the Swiss government, you simply stole from the Swiss government, you'd better remember that, he said. And besides, I know that they changed the currency in your country, he said, and you came with the old money. His eyes glittered when he said this. I only want your own good, you must understand that, only your own good, he said.

After that there was a long corridor with the only other person sitting in it a strange hulking boy with strange wild eyes making savage noises. He had a shirt painted in shining colors, all peacocks with their tails open, and peacocks tattooed on his wrists. He asked her what she had done. She didn't answer. He laughed a mean laugh.

You didn't kill anyone, he said.

She didn't answer.

He said: You stole something in a supermarket, you stole panties in a supermarket.

She didn't answer.

For panties in a supermarket you rot in jail here, he said. The Swiss hate it when you take panties from the supermarkets. It's a big deal for the Swiss, panties in a supermarket—just don't lie, they'll tell you.

He fixed her with his eyes and the mean laughter burst out of his whole body which shifted nervously on the chair.

. . .

And they took me in, she said. The clock on the wall said four. The Examining Magistrate said he was supposed to be home at four-fifteen and his wife didn't like him to be late. He would have to phone and tell her he was coming late. Of course, said Herr Zutter and the Examining Magistrate phoned his wife that he'd be ten minutes late because he had a little problem here. After that he said something and typed on a typewriter. She didn't hear what he said, only the typewriter, looking first at his typing hands and then at the wall above him, with posters of Klee and Mondrian and a still life with a guitar by Braque. The Examining Magistrate typed rapidly and she answered the questions and said *Yes yes* looking at the Braque guitar all the time. He said they would have to get it over quickly and she understood that if they got it over quickly the little problem might grow even littler, and in the window the blue was cobalt and she said to herself that soon she would be lying on her bed in the hotel and looking at the ceiling and tomorrow she would get on a tram and ride and ride and ride all day. The cobalt blue became ultramarine. Silence fell. Again she repeated to herself that what the Swiss liked was the truth and what they hated was a lie, and Herr Zutter said say *Yes* and she said *Yes*. Repeat after me, said the Examining Magistrate. And she repeated after him. He asked if she had anything to say. She didn't answer. You have nothing to say, he said and asked if it was necessary to translate because he was in a hurry. She shook her head, no there was no need to translate, but the Examining Magistrate said it wasn't enough to shake her head it was a protocol and she had to say *Yes* to go into the protocol and she said *Yes* to go into the protocol. Her jaws were swollen. Her cheekbones hurt. And she felt her neck swelling and its volume expanding every time she said *Yes*. She tried in vain to stretch her neck, holding a block of wood between her head and shoulders, a block of wood full of sawdust getting thicker and thicker. *Yes,* she said, feeling the block of sawdust going down from her neck to her chest and from her chest to her stomach and down to the pit of her stomach and something hollow and heavy moving round in her body. The Examining Magistrate gave her the paper and told her to sign. She took it, looking at the Braque guitar, and signed. The Examining Magistrate said: *Ja,* he was already five minutes late, his wife didn't like it at all when he was five minutes late, and showing signs of panic he slipped into his coat and snatched his umbrella and ran, and Herr Zutter told her to wait because

it was already late and the Examining Magistrate had only written a report without deciding anything definite and in Switzerland it had to be
definite, and he told her to go back to the corridor and she sat down
again next to the boy with the brightly colored peacocks and the mean
laugh but now he didn't look at her he just sat there stinking of tobacco,
and then he let out a meaningful grunt and began voraciously scratching
his hands. The corridor was brightly lit. In the big window red and yellow gleamed and the ultramarine turned into indigo. She stretched her
legs. The boy with the mean laugh made a peculiar noise again, looking
at her from his seat, and then the policeman came and said let's go.
Where to, she asked. For a ride, he said and told her to get in and
pushed her inside and she sat down and they drove through the streets
with the trams and the shops and the lamps and the people with the
plastic bags, and then they turned into other streets and it was quiet and
it was raining. A procession of priests walked past in the rain. She listened to the rain beating down on the cobblestones. The streets smelled
exciting and she looked at them, squinting with wild desire. The streets
raced. The trams raced. The cars raced. There were sounds of traffic in the
street, sounds of traffic in the air and bells rang for prayer, bells of glass
of iron of branches and trees. She listened, squinting wildly, wanting
wildly to be joined to the racing world, the real running racing world, to
be joined to the windows, the blinds, the neon signs, the black revolving glass doors. In the café entrances magic lights and red lamps flickered, in this direction, in that. The noise increased. The car bumped forward and backward and she was thrown forward and backward and they
stopped and told her to get out and she got out and someone pushed
her lightly and told her to go in and next to the counter they asked her if
she had anything else on her and she said she had nothing on her, nothing, nothing, she said, but the man behind the counter didn't look at her
and didn't answer her, and two policemen came in and told her to come
and started marching fast down corridors of nailed metal walls between
nailed metal doors. The block of wood was already inside her feet and
she marched slowly, unable to lift her feet, and they pushed her and
shouted *weiter, weiter*. She asked where to but they shouted *weiter weiter*
and took her down in a metal elevator to a huge metal room and sat her
down on a metal chair and turned her head and snapped and snapped
again and after that they told her to press her thumb and she pressed her
thumb and they told her to press the palm of her hand and she pressed
and they moved her palm on the plate and turned the chair round and

put her palm on the plate again and she said: They told me that if I signed I could go home, and they shouted *weiter* and marched her down the nailed metal corridors with the nailed doors and she shrieked wildly that they told her she could go home and she wouldn't go with them. I want to know where I am, she shrieked, and they caught her by both hands and dragged her along the iron floor down the long corridors of the huge prison and she shrieked I won't go, I won't go, and two huge men held her by both arms and dragged her along the floor and they reached an iron door and opened the iron door and pushed her inside and shut the iron door. And I was a prisoner, she said.

About the jail I don't know much. She said little and what she said was confused, the way people talk about a time that resembles a hallucination or a nightmare, trying to report the facts but afraid of showing her hand, as if playing for stakes that were too high, and when I try to reconstruct the story it sounds more or less like this: She beat against the iron door with her fists. A voice answered, thunderous like drums. She beat again, with both fists. The iron thundered, coming back from other walls and answering from countless doors along the corridors, hitting the floors above and the floors below with a renewed metallic clang. She heard footsteps in the corridor. The footsteps approached. Then they receded. The iron voice died away. She beat again, savagely, raving. The shrill swooping shrieks of a mighty flock of cymbals answered. She went on beating, with clenched fists, furiously, feeling the blood pouring from her fists and streaming slowly down her arms. She felt the dampness on her arms under her sleeves, but she went on beating, hopping up and down like a little animal. The footsteps approached and receded and approached and receded again. She stopped for a minute, listening. Muffled voices came back from the empty spaces and the corridors, voices drawn out in a long low trumpet call. She began beating again, demented, hitting her fists on the iron door, hearing the iron orchestra answer, zigzagging down the corridors, breaking somewhere down below and coming back with every new blow of her fists. She went on, beating, beating, she felt enormous strength in her hands and opened her bleeding hands. For a moment she looked at them, astounded, but still she felt enormous strength in her hands and she opened her palms and beat the iron with her palms, with the delicate skin of her palms, which was immediately scratched and burning, but still she felt enormous strength in her hands and she opened her fingers and began to beat with her fingers. She felt a fierce pain in her fingers, in the skin and the little joints, and that her fingers were breaking, but still she felt enormous strength in her hands and she turned her fingers round, beating with the hard side of her fingers. The footsteps in the corridor approached and receded and approached and receded. The cymbals suddenly grew low, children's cymbals, almost toy cymbals, and she lifted the wounded palms of her hands to her eyes, examining the raw exposed flesh, the pink flesh of a fresh burn. The madness intensified and she began beating with her forehead, feeling her forehead deep in the bones of her temples. Thin trickles of blood dripped into her eyes, and she closed her eyes which were full of bloody tears. She wiped the reddish liquid from her eyes, feeling in the depths of her face the two painful balls hollow like two inverted pockets. The reddish liquid went on flowing, dripping onto the balls of her fingers, and she pushed her fingers into her hair, drawing them backwards, wanting to wipe the balls of her fingers as she tried to stand still for a minute, but on both sides of her face two enormous ears protruded, growing bigger from minute to minute, growing more remote from her face and more alien. She moved her head to one side. Then to the other. But the enormous ears moved somewhere far from her head, heavy, full of strange sounds of tools and hammers and saws and grating sounds of shattering glass, and she pressed her back to the iron door, beating now with her back. The hammers stopped and so did the saws, the cymbals and the trumpet, and now she heard only the grating sound of shattering glass, the scraping sound of fingernails on hard stone, the sounds of things moving and rustling. She went on beating her back against the door, trying to raise her hands, feeling the thin muddy trickles making warm little pools in her armpits, and she went on slamming her back on the door, but the blows now reached her ears dimly, like the muffled bellow of a wounded animal. She began to scream, raving, beating alternately with her forehead, her skull, her back, hearing the sounds of her thudding body coming back to her from the walls and from the corridors surrounding her like a vast barrel. The pain in her hands grew piercing, and she lifted them and pressed them to her face, tightening her face, and then she felt the terrible chill spreading through her body.

It was already dark in the peephole when she saw a crack and in the crack stood a warden. He asked if she was the one banging. She said she wanted them to inform the consul. He smiled kindly. He said: What consul? My country's, she said. He smiled again, kindly. He said that a prisoner had no consul, and pushed her back inside. She said that she demanded a lawyer. He smiled again, kindly. He had small round glasses with pale steel frames, and he raised the glasses a little, smiling. What you can do is rot here, he said smiling and pushed her inside so hard that she fell on the floor. Her face was bleeding and she wiped the blood with her skirt.

The cell was all stone, yellowish-grey, and looked like a tomb, and there was an iron door in the tomb, and a bed and a lavatory and a light bulb hanging from the ceiling. And maybe not a tomb, maybe something like a dog's kennel, only higher, she said.

And then the nightmare began, when she sat down on the bed.

Her face was blank when she told me this, leaving her at moments with an expression of shock, as if something sudden had fallen next to her face which was very pale, burning with a sickly pallor. She looked at me now in silence, not taking her eyes off me, eyes glittering but cold, an iron cold, blue-grey, a steely cold, and I thought that perhaps she could still hear the chords and metallic sounds here in the park, at a lower octave. For a moment it seemed to me that I could hear them too, and the closed echo zigzagging. She went on looking at me, her face faintly illuminated by the lamp above the bench, which illuminated small, rather chubby hands, almost a child's hands, and suddenly I remembered the wide illuminated trams, the sausages and mustard, the long slender pears, the fruit rotten at the core and the hard winter I had spent in Zurich roaming the long streets, standing at night in empty stations, freezing in my little Israeli fur, leaning against the walls of the houses with the statues of monsters, of lions and tigers, looking for a pair of wings to shelter me, looking for a God to pray to, and a man standing next to me at the empty tram station, an elegantly dressed man with an umbrella bent over me with his umbrella: You shouldn't look at the empty tracks, Madam, he said, anyone who looks at the empty tracks will die, Madam.

You were thinking about something, she said.

I denied it. I said I was listening. Her mouth twisted in an embarrassed grin, and for a moment she crossed her hands behind her back, then she put them back on her knees, stretching her legs and looking at me intently, her head lowered, stubbornly examining my face again. Of course you were thinking about something, she said. I denied it again, ignoring the signs of violence in her voice. She moved her shoulders, shuddering for a moment as if an electric current were running through her body, and went on as if there had been no interruption. Well, she said, and then I noticed the fresco.

Then the nightmare began, when she sat down on the bed. Then she noticed the fresco on the walls, a huge colorful fresco of names and writing and huge swollen penises that were drawn on all the walls, red penises and green penises and black penises and white and yellow and upside-down and cut-off and squashed-up penises, drawn with thick shining crayons and charcoal and chalk and iodine, as well as coffee and soup and blood. Most of them weren't joined to any body or coming out of any body, but hanging from a little hairy triangle, which looked like medallions for hanging bathroom towels or kitchen towels, and only here and there they were sticking out of tiny little flattened-out bodies, like cartoon bodies. She looked, frightened, stunned, trying to read the names that were written in huge clumsy letters in Arabic and English and French, making out something like Abdalla or Hafez or Asad or Charlie or John, and trying to decipher the writing, but the monstrous penises swelled emerging from the walls advancing on her on her body. She began to shake. The hundred-headed monster came apart and the wall suddenly filled up with gigantic lizards covered in stocky hairy skin, and she heard the terrible swarming, she felt the hairy skin in her mouth and a revolting nausea. She went on sitting, clinging to the railing of the bed, but the hundred-headed monster came apart again. The lizards turned into snakes, and she saw them clearly advancing on her, on her body, slimy, hissing, closing in on her and climbing up her and coiling round her neck and crawling into her throat and filling her mouth and her throat and choking her inside her throat. She felt the bundles of flesh and blood, she felt gaping jaws and tongues and teeth and gaping jaws and tongues and teeth swelling without stopping, attached to gigantic bladders swelling without stopping, turning into frightening tumors covered with hard animal skin. She gazed terrified at the infinite expansion, gripping the railing of the bed, trying to get up and failing. The monsters moved, clinging to the wall. Then they crawled out of the wall. Everything whirled in a crazy vertigo. The nausea, the terror, the snakes and dragons, the throttled birds, the handles and the axes, the soft flesh and hard animal skin, and she felt a terrible pain in her stomach and heard a growling in her stomach and the gigantic penises writhing inside her stomach and she jumped off the bed, trying to stand and leaning against the lavatory. But all around her strange black wings moved with slender bones moved with nails and claws and she saw the ceiling getting lower and narrower, she smelled burning rubber and charred tires, the smell of the yellowish liquid in the lavatory bowl. She began a frantic jig. Her stomachache grew worse. The demented arabesque moved up and down up and down whirling in a carousel in the narrow illuminated den with the ceiling getting lower and narrower all the time and now she could see the letters clearly, the coats, the capes, the hooks and axes, she could see Ahmed and Hafez and Muhamad and Salah and Charlie and John and she felt a terrible force digging into her eyes ripping her eyes from her head. From the corridor came a vicious laugh. After that there was a scream. The gigantic penises swelled choking her throat and she vomited her guts onto the floor.

No, I can't talk about that night, she said.

The light bulb on the ceiling burned all night. She tried to wrap herself in the blanket but there was an appalling stench coming from the blanket, and she lay frozen, wide-eyed, looking at the light bulb. From the neighboring cells she heard tapping. She didn't answer. The tapping was repeated. She didn't answer. Fear turned her body into a petrified lump and she could hardly turn over or lie on her side, staring wide-eyed at the light bulb on the ceiling. She asked herself if it was raining. Perhaps there was a storm. Yes, there was surely a storm. And she was here, what misery, what wretched misery, and she would die here, alone, misjudged, and forgotten, alone and forgotten, and no one would ever know, no one would ever look for her, even when they began to worry at home and Gerda would say: Where's Rutchen what's happened to Rutchen why doesn't she call, and he would grunt or growl something into the green oilcloth.

This is where I'll remain, this is where I'll be buried, she said and sat up in a panic. The bed was high, and she sat, sweating, in the freezing cold, not connected to anything, in the air, at a great height, a terrifyingly great height. The tapping on the walls was repeated, tapping from the neighboring cells, from the corridors, from the elevators, from the iron doors. She tried to think who was here yesterday who was locked up on the other side of the wall tonight. She thought she heard murmurs on the other side of the wall in the neighboring cell, the murmurs of murderers, thieves, rapists, scorpions and nails. Her hands were frozen and she tried to warm them in vain, saying to herself that there was nothing to be afraid of, no murmurs were coming from the neighboring cell, no noises could penetrate these walls, no blows no hopes no fears. She felt a momentary relief, protected. From the frescoed wall opposite she heard a loud tapping, getting faster all the time. She listened. For a moment it seemed to her that she understood. The tapping was repeated more slowly, almost gently, almost warmly. It seemed to her that there were groans coming from the other side of the wall and someone on the other side of the wall was crying or singing. She listened intently, shaking all over. Somewhere in the distance a church chimed three chimes. She said: No, not chimes, it was eagles flying, three eagles flying. Now she remembered Herr Zutter saying something about a hurricane and she said: No, there aren't any hurricanes at home, why did he ask about a hurricane? No, it's the rain, it's a storm, there's a storm blowing, the trees are going wild outside, everything's flying outside, there's lightning outside. Suddenly she remembered how everything had happened, the empty bag gaping wide and being dragged down the corridors like a rabbit, like a little animal. She pressed her eyelids hard, searching for the snapped thread of lucidity. Her heart beat like a drum and she inclined her head to the wall next to the bed. But it was silent. Everything gradually froze. Everything was death. And she would remain here. She would be buried here. She tried to revive her hands.

But that's impossible, of course I won't be buried here, she said. There was a moldy smell in the cell, a smell of damp earth, of flesh and bones, a smell of unknown, decomposing bodies, and she said to herself: These must be the prisoners who died here, people must have died here. The saliva turned into a thick paste between her teeth and she clamped her teeth together. These are the prisoners who died here, she said, this is the smell of the prisoners who died here, the ones the warders found here dead in the morning, hanging on the gigantic penises in the morning, on the bundles of snakes on the empty jaws on the sheets on the strips of flesh. She trembled, bracing her arms at the sides of her body, trying to sit, but suddenly she jumped up and stood, suddenly she saw herself running, she was quite certain of it, she saw herself running in the corridors, in the empty courtyards, she was quite certain of it, in the windows and on the walls, flat against the walls and running,

running, crushed in the carousel with the gigantic whirling penises, plummeting in the muddy air in the gaping barrel stuffed into the lizards, the snakes, the network of canals, the names and the eyes, the dancing demons, the cartoon bodies, the sour stench and the writing soiled with excrement. She felt such terrible nausea that she was forced to cling to the walls, pressing against the huge swollen maleness, and suddenly she felt that she was bleeding, it wasn't her time yet but she was bleeding, suddenly she felt the blood dripping dirty from her body between her legs as if from an open belly. She moved her legs. Everything was sticky, her panties, her skirt, her stockings, everything was full of the thick stale mud and the sour smell of blood. She raised it to her face, sniffing, feeling it hot on her skin. Her dirty, superfluous blood poured out of her interspersed with little lumps of glue, always too early always too late, and how life had stupefied her, and it was dark outside, outside the wind raced, the air was full of ink outside, and how thin her naked knees were, how strange, what short legs full of thin trickles of blood and red sweat, and she was a bleeding animal, that's what she was, an animal bleeding between its legs, that's what I am, she said. She had on a black skirt and she took it off. There was a big stain of black on black. The smell was unbearable. The skin between her legs was chafed and she thought she would get undressed and sit naked, but the cold was terrible, the writing on the wall grew bigger and so did the shiny colored penises embedded in the walls and passing through the walls and she felt their presence inside the walls and inside the floor opening the belly of the floor felt the hair in her mouth the smell of the urine of yesterday and Abdalla and Hafez and Asad and Charlie and John none of them bled, not from their legs, and she bled, that's what she was, an animal bleeding between its legs, she said.

She felt a weakness in her knees, in her feet and toes, with a prickling in the toes, and said to herself that the blood wasn't reaching her legs, she tried to lift her legs sitting high up on the iron bed. But they dangled, dropped, resisting her efforts, as if they were strapped down. Suddenly she felt a passionate desire to touch the floor, and she jumped on the floor, hearing the thudding of her feet on the floor. Her feet were hard. The echo was strong. And she felt something strong some strong invisible force coming from the floor and going straight into her feet. Again there were footsteps in the corridor. The light bulb burned like a little sun and she realized that it would never go out, it would go on beating on her eyes forever, and she didn't know which was worse, the darkness or the light. She climbed onto the bed, she stood on the bed, trying to reach the light, but it was fixed into the ceiling, and she heard her own footsteps in the cell, with no day, no night, no watch, inside some eternal calendar. The silver ball opposite her eyes blazed, and something like laughter writhed inside her body, struggling in her stomach like an animal inside a sack. Suddenly she remembered reading stories in the newspapers about Israelis rotting in jails all over the world, in Amsterdam, Stockholm, Munich, New York, for taking drugs, selling drugs, and she, coins, coins, she exchanged small change.

And still it was something without substance, without meaning. She stretched out her hands, as if freeing herself from a trap, and looked at me intently, with a sudden strength pulling in the opposite direction. There was a desolate expression on her face, as if something had happened, as if she had suddenly sensed the slow dissolution of time.

That's it, and then it happened, she said, then she felt her whole body like a tattoo, she felt the ink inside her skin and the smell of stale herring in her skin. Her hands were blue. Her body long. And long snakes with tiny heads crawled in the ink on the long body, rustling like paper butterflies, O God, paper butterflies, and she stared and stared, the two empty balls hurt her deep inside her face but she stared and stared and the little sun that would never, O God never, go out again burned over her. The cell was white. The fresco passed in procession. Quiet. Moving with an imperceptible tremor and white as white could be, it too illuminated by the light of the little sun that would never, O God never, go out again, and she was here, O God, she was here alone, and there was no God, no coins, no father, no people in the world, no sound came from anywhere no living soul and only the trumpet imitating the sound of weeping. A new fountain of vomit spewed from her throat. She screamed. Someone tapped on the other side of the wall. The snakes reared to the ceiling. The tattoo netting on her body burned like an inflammation. And then it came to her, the demented desire to write on the walls, she said. She looked at me, blinking her eyes as if they were out of her control, as if now too she felt the ink netting her body. She asked if I knew what she wanted to write. I said I didn't know. She laughed quietly, shocked by her laughter. She said: For example, what's the connection between lie and die, that was the first sentence. She asked if I knew what came after that. I asked what. She laughed again, quiet, shocked by her laughter. There was this one verse stuck in my head, she said, it simply flew onto the walls like a soul flies. I looked at her. I didn't ask what. There was a kind of passion of revenge in her voice, but her face was completely blank and expressionless and only her eyes darted over me, now shining, almost radiant, as if held by two silver tacks.

She laughed nervously.

You'll never guess, she said and laughed nervously.

Her words became more and more confused, and from the few confused words I understood that first she searched for her eyebrow pencil and undid all her pockets and linings, but there was nothing in the pockets and nothing in the lining, and she turned the lining inside out and stuck her fingers into the seams but there was nothing in the seams either, and then she tried with her nails but it didn't come out with her nails, and then she wrote in her blood, opening her legs and dipping, and she wrote it big, round, the width of her finger, you know it, she said. She fixed me with the two silver tacks again. You know it, she said again. Her face was very white now and only her cheeks burned like two painted poppies. She coughed dryly. Now too I didn't ask what. She still coughed dryly. You'll never guess, she said again, casting nervous glances over her shoulder, as if she was sitting high above the floor like then, and that solitude, that loneliness, was still groaning in the stifling sourness, the words running through the air around her, smearing big, round, the width of her finger, smearing: AND I WAS LEFT NAKED AND BARE, that's it, you'll never guess, she repeated for the third time, big, round, the width of her finger, on all the walls, what a celebration, AND I WAS LEFT NAKED AND BARE AND FOR THESE THINGS I WEEP AND I WAS LEFT NAKED AND BARE AND FOR THESE THINGS I WEEP AND I WAS LEFT NAKED AND BARE AND FOR THESE THINGS I WEEP, you see, I'm not right in the head, she said. Her face was green and she held her hands so tight against her face that it looked as if she had nails on her face. There, between the giant colored penises, between Abdalla and Hafez and Asad and Charlie and John, AND FOR THESE THINGS I WEEP, do you think I'm crazy, she said.

The lamp above the bench shed a sandy color on her hair and she pushed her feet into the damp sparkling grass. Then she tucked them up on the bench. There was a silly smile on her face, a horrifying, almost imploring smile. She was silent for a moment, gathering her strength. And I wanted to write something else, she said. Again I didn't ask what. And again the same silly, almost imploring, almost horrifying smile spread over her face. She said: Something like the Golem, to run raving in the streets like the Golem, to lie here raving like the Golem, to break the walls, raving, like the Golem, a lifeless formless man. She spoke now without looking at me and I felt the words gnawing her, and that solitude, that loneliness, looking for the tattoo on her body. You can never reach the end of the snake, she said. She was still holding her hands to her face. And I wanted to write *their throat is an open sepulcher* too, she said, you know what I mean.

There was a silence. I didn't know what to say. She smiled. Of course you know, she said. I didn't know what to say. I said yes, I knew what she meant. But you were thinking about something else, she said. I said yes, I was thinking about something else. She didn't ask what. It isn't true, you were thinking about *their throat is an open sepulcher,* she said. She was still speaking without looking at me. Every woman knows it, she said. Now too I didn't know what to say. I said yes, every woman knows, and I suddenly saw the fresco in yellow in black in raspberry red moving on the trees, on the back of the trunks, on the barrels and the damp grass, I saw the snakes rearing, the blind birds, the immense swollen maleness, the forest of black beams, the black cylinders, the total darkness eclipsing thought. I remembered the story about my friend in the Brooklyn subway, how she had once gone down at night to the deserted station and three little black demons had jumped out of the corners and pushed a sweating black fist into her mouth into her throat and thrown her down onto the platform of the deserted station and raped her one after the other with the fist in her throat and a train came and stopped and went away and came again and stopped and went away and the three little demons went on the fist in her throat and ran away leaving her in torn clothes and torn legs torn between her legs with her throat an open sepulcher.

She looked at me. Her voice blazed.

I heard there are men who make a woman do it in the throat, she said.

I said I didn't know.

You never read about it? she said.

I said perhaps, I didn't know.

I knew a woman like that, she said, all her life she walked around with an open sepulcher. She never ate, only vomited.

She looked at me again, very concentrated.

You vomit in your soul, she said.

Sometimes, I said.

Her face turned the color of ink.

In your soul, she said.

Sometimes, I said.

She laughed a cold bitter laugh.

Oh, no, there in the cell, with the fresco, and what was crawling over the floor, what was crawling from the walls, from behind the walls, they couldn't have known there was a woman sitting there, but they knew, they sensed it through the walls, they masturbated through the walls, Abdalla and Hafez and Asad and Charlie and John, I felt their gigantic penises poking through the walls and the spittle and the terrible smell, I saw the holes come alive. Suddenly she was silent, shrinking on the bench. I couldn't even eat: It jumped at me from the filthy coffee from the dreadful soup, she said. She looked at me desperately, Oh, no, she said. Now her face was completely expressionless with big beads of sweat breaking out on it like drops of hot rain.

About birds of prey, she said suddenly. Her voice sounded strange, a whistling sound, and she pressed her back up hard against the bench again. There's only one bird of prey, she said: Your thoughts.

And it was she of course who lit the fire, a few days after her return. How long she spent in jail I don't know, and how she got out she told me only afterwards, when we were sitting on the concrete wall next to the house. The air was so still that we heard Gerda's soft moans coming clearly from the balcony, high-pitched, with a shrill sound like a tin whistle. Rutchen pretended to be deaf. She was always a wheezer, even when I was a child, she said. She didn't turn round to look through the window, although the head bobbing in there was visible from where we sat, and the whistling through the cracked pipe didn't stop. She said: How she swings there in the window. It really looked as if the head were swinging, hanging on the gathered pink curtain from a scrawny pink neck, its jaws sticking out like a skull. I remembered that she was once a beautiful woman with beautiful high cheekbones and how I had liked watching her when she stood at the window. The shrill whistling went on, monotonous, irritating. It was hard to listen. Through the nylon curtain two deep holes of despair poked out and then you could see the pink fabric flapping as if torn and the two holes of despair sinking into some dark pit. Gerda had apparently turned off the light and sat down. Rutchen looked at me, perhaps reading my thoughts. You see, like a skull, she said. There was open hostility in her voice. She said: Oh, no, he won't leave her, he'll haunt her after death, he won't leave her. From behind the window the lifeless mask went on swaying down low and the tin whistle wailed. Rutchen looked, hard. Oh, no, he won't leave her, she repeated, he's like the rain, like the wind, he won't leave her. She stood for a moment, listening. Suddenly she turned to me. She'll still feel his hands, she said.

The sight in the window was rather unnerving. Again Gerda popped up, shaking her head as if trying at long last to fly out of the window. Rutchen asked again if I knew the story about the cat. A passing car lit her face in a sudden wash of brightness. She blinked both eyes. Then she returned to the subject of the jail, but how long she spent there I couldn't begin to understand. What I understood was only that they let her out on the day she had a plane ticket home. And that was my luck, she said. It was Herr Zutter who explained it to her. He said that the Swiss government didn't have to waste a plane ticket on her. It was early in the morning. They opened the cell door early in the morning and Herr Zutter was waiting for her below. He asked if everything had been returned to her. Then he asked what she had had. Here's the parcel, check and see, he said. She said it was all right. But Herr Zutter said: No, it's not all right, you must check, and she checked. The ring was there, and the watch. In her purse everything was arranged the way it was before, the bundles of small change too, and rolled up in a little bundle was the shame. That was what she said to them when she came home. In silver foil, wrapped and twisted on top, only she didn't remember if it was in the bundles of tens or fives, and it was then that he cried quietly, quietly, she said, it was then that he cried, and she said: And in the seams of the skirt that I undid, and in the lining, and he cried, and she turned the lining inside out, and then she turned the pockets inside out, and he, his fingers were crawling over his face, but she repeated it, and how I tore the pockets, she said, how I tore the pockets, how I came back, you see, Papa, with the small change, the small change, that's what I brought, the small change, and he cried, and she said: You're falling asleep, Papa, you're fast asleep, why are you keeping your fingers on your face, Papa, and his face, to see his face, crumpled like crumpled paper, but she kept on: And what did you write on your sick chart, Papa, what did you write on your sick chart, and he, suddenly lean, sharp-eyed, his hair on end: What sick chart? Your sick chart, Papa, your sick chart, you were a driver, Papa, have you forgotten that you were a driver that you were always looking at the road, that you had eyes, you remember that you ran over dogs on the road that you ran over cats, that you drove over squashed bodies, and he didn't move, and where are you looking, where are you looking, Papa, and he didn't move, he said: Nowhere, I'm not looking anywhere, and he wasn't crying any more.

Suddenly she was silent.

Yes, he wasn't looking anywhere, she said. She asked what the time was. Her voice was wooden. I forgot that they gave me my watch back, she said. I listened to her wooden voice. She was silent again. You think the watch is holy? she said and she was silent again. She looked weak, tired and stupefied, as if she was still hearing her own voice and how that cruel conversation went on day after day. The silence lengthened, and I saw him suddenly, his face really crumpled like crumpled paper, opening the empty albums, fingering the empty cellophane paper and turning the pages, turning the pages, and the evil spirit haunting the house, and him turning the pages, turning the pages, I remembered Rutchen's wild laughter and Gerda: Stop it, that's enough, take pity on the child, but he kept on turning the pages, turning the pages, and Rutchen, inside the bubble of light, looking, and in the huge department store the people peering behind her back ran, heads with parcels ran, the slanting little television screens on the ceiling ran, the dent in her father's chin ran, the cellophane pages in the empty albums ran, the rolls of silver foil the monstrous figures clinging to the walls, the strong hands carrying her—You think the watch is holy? she said again. Now too her voice was dry. That's it, that's what it all adds up to in the end, she said.

The cat's name was Pudding, but Shlezi called it "The Inheritance." The Inheritance is hungry, he said. Or: The Inheritance is bawling again. Sometimes he said: The Inheritance is waiting. He, at any rate, was not going to leave any cats to his daughter, and he was going to write it in his will too, he said, it would be written in his will. And sometimes he added: I'm changing it next week, you know. And when neither of the women showed any curiosity he repeated: Yes, yes, next week. But Gerda was crazy about the cat, the one he ran over later on. She really had inherited it from her mother, who really did leave it to her in her will, and in fact that was the entire will, because when she died she took everything with her except for the cat, which had a name as sweet as Pudding and also a yellow body and a flabby belly that Shlezi hated. In its yellow body were two yellow eyes that drew Gerda, bewitched her and this too Shlezi hated, and although Pudding was always guzzling it had a look of permanent hunger and you could say that Shlezi hated this, too. He said that Gerda, like the cat, had a look of permanent hunger, and what was it she lacked, what was it she lacked, always leaning against the door, always silent never answering. She really did lean against the door, pressing her cheek to it hard, and it was impossible to tell from her face if she heard. The only one she talked to sometimes was the cat, who followed her wherever she went, to the street, to the kitchen, to the store, or lay next to her pressed against the door, looking at her with that hungry look, a look that tore her soul to pieces, and this too Shlezi hated. But more than anything he hated it when it jumped onto his stamp album. It jumped onto my stamp album, he yelled, raving, his eyes meeting as if he had one eye under his forehead.

People told a lot of stories about the cat, especially how once, when it jumped onto the stamp album, Shlezi tied it to a pole and ran over it. Then he drove backward a bit. After that he drove forward a bit again. After that he left the mangled lump of flesh on the road and went inside. He jumped onto my stamp album, he said. There was another version too, Mr. "Everything Cheap"'s version, for instance. He said that he simply smashed the cat in half, he bashed it and bashed it until it popped. Only the head, whole, flew to the electricity pole, cut right along the seam. He saw it with his own eyes, how the head flew to the electricity pole. He trembled with excitement when he told it. Aiming the wheels like that, he said, aiming the wheels of a bus to cut like a kitchen knife, right along the seam. Because "Mr. Everything Cheap" suffered from asthma he had to take a deep breath, and he took a deep breath and calmed down. Incredible, you could actually see its yellow eyes jumping out and spinning round, he said after he calmed down. But Mrs. Klein told it a little differently. She said that he took an orange crate and tied the cat up inside the crate. Then he tied the crate to a tree and started the bus. They heard the tree creak and after that the dreadful howl of the cat, and then he drove backward a bit, and after that forward a bit again. She liked adding that he left a few oranges in the crate and they stayed whole next to the crushed body, only their color was no longer orange. She also liked adding that Gerda, pale as death, made some dry little sounds, but Shlezi yelled: Yes, he jumped onto my

stamp album, can't you see? And Gerda went on standing there, para-
lyzed, her neck twisted backwards and her jaw dropping. She couldn't
understand what he was talking about.

That's what Mrs. Klein said, said Rutchen. She asked me if I hadn't
heard. I said I hadn't heard. She shrugged her shoulders. That's impossible, she said. Then she said that Mrs. Klein also liked adding that he
had run her over, too, over Gerda, crushed her slowly, without a bus
and without a road, on the chair, sitting up. He had put her neck in the
plaster cast right from the start. Yes, that's what Mrs. Klein said. She
asked if I hadn't heard that either. Nasty, she said, but a fact. She waited
a minute, as if something important had slipped her memory. And my
father did that, she said. He was a quiet man. He was even a good man.
He had always worried about her a lot. But it was after that that Gerda
stopped talking. She said this quietly. There was a kind of horror in her
voice. She asked if he had told me the story about the cats that ate each
other. I said he hadn't told me. She said: Really? Really? And, smiling
incredulously, repeated the story about the cats that ate one another
alive leaving only their tails behind them. She smiled incredulously
again. He can't possibly never have told you that, she said. Her upper
lip quivered slightly. She said: Papa loved that story. He was always telling it to Ma as a joke, but she never laughed at the joke. She looked at
me incredulously again. He can't never have told you that, she repeated. Then she said that once he had brought Gerda some cheese
with a picture of a laughing head of a cat and after that Gerda never ate
cheese again. Her face burned when she told me this, and she stared at
me with pale, sweating, almost yellow eyes, and bent over the stone
wall beating on the stone. After that Gerda never ate cheese again, she
repeated. The simple words sounded strange in her mouth and she
went on hitting the stone. Can a wall give grapes? she suddenly said.
Her face was still burning and there was a strange ring in her voice.
Walls don't give grapes, she said wildly and burst out crying.

I looked at her. It was a soft whimper, a kind of whine unconnected
to time or place or any particular event. Upstairs the telephone rang
and went on ringing. Gerda didn't answer. She was still standing in the
window, still swaying as if she wanted to fly out of the window. Since
the room was dark her face was brightly lit, casting a long, vulturous
shadow. Her hair was tied wildly around her head and you could see it
falling sideways against the window frame and her neck moving heavily
in the plaster cast. Rutchen swallowed her tears, sinking into her place

on the stone again. It seemed to me she said something, but I didn't hear what she said. Low clouds came down on the street, after that a figure emerged inside them and a clearly legible word appeared. After that the figure disappeared and only the word remained, hanging in the air in the low dense mist, but it was hard to read the word. Rutchen said something again, but again I didn't hear what she said. A young man walked down the street whistling a very pretty, merry tune. She raised herself and watched him heading away. He was wearing a shining black coat and his steps were very soft and so was the merry tune receding into the distance. In the meantime the decor changed and the sky suddenly grew high, opening into the high air, full of disembodied stories creeping over the balconies and over the roofs. Then the mist like a soft sponge blotted out the roofs. The streets looked like deep crevices. The mountain was full of wind, and the air was shaken by a mighty voice, whose source was hard to tell. It's going to rain, said Rutchen and turned toward the window where Gerda's head still loomed whitely, but now she seemed amazingly calm, standing in some distant time in some alien existence. Her face looked very big and very white, emphasizing the coal black of her hair, and even in the darkness you could see her look of permanent hunger. Rutchen observed her with intense attention. Papa used to say that once people used to have funerals in the evening, for the air, she said. Her voice was almost compassionate and her lips trembled like the lips of a sick child, as if she wanted to cry her heart out. She stiffened again and turned sharply toward me. Her mouth twisted wryly. That's it, what's left is the small change, she said and rubbed her hands as if they were stained with her own blood.

The young man in the shining black coat came back again, whistling the merry tune. She mumbled something, wanting perhaps to get into conversation, but he apparently didn't notice us sitting on the stone fence, and she watched him move away in the opposite direction, her eyes fixed on his back in the shining black coat, repeating slightly off-key the tune that sounded even better off-key, enriched with a grotesque melancholy sound. It was clear that somewhere, behind her, in the window, the silence had deepened, and she turned her head slowly round to face the window, where Gerda was still standing with elongated limbs and a face of wax. Her hands were spread out, holding onto the window frame, making the shape of a cross in the window. It seemed as if behind the cross, in the darkness, there were other, invisible windows, and other hands multiplied there, holding on to the frames.

Rutchen turned round, still whistling off-key, swaying slowly and pensively in time to the tune. In the meantime the telephone stopped ringing and it was silent inside. She asked if I had ever been in jail. I said no. Strange, she said. A couple coming down the steps, out of the house into the street, passed us, very deep in conversation. The man spoke quietly to the woman. He said: The orchestra began playing and they hanged him and the rope broke and they brought another rope and it broke again and they hanged him again and the orchestra went on playing. We said we wouldn't talk, we said we'd walk without talking, said the woman. Rutchen apparently caught only the last words. Her face was burning now like fire. With Ma it took years, the madness of not talking, she said.

She lit the fire, as I said before, a few days after her return. They weren't in the house, of course, or more precisely they were at the other end of the house in "Mr. Everything Cheap"'s flat, having their weekly game of cards. It was a boring game, and Shlezi was particularly apathetic, brooding and withdrawn and not his usual self. He was wearing his working clothes, although he was no longer a bus driver, and they looked as if they weren't his, hanging clumsily on his body. He forgot to sweeten his coffee and drank it bitter, letting it get cold, pulling a face with every sip as if he were drinking poison. His remarks were mean, his face sour, and whenever he threw down a card he sank absentmindedly into the armchair, as if the pile of cards was disintegrating in front of his eyes, which were bleary and half-shut. Then he got up and left before the end, and Gerda of course followed him. The two flats were joined by a long passage, and already in the passage they could sense something suspicious and a charred smell, and Gerda thought that the toaster element had burnt out. It had already happened several times before that the toaster element had burnt out, usually causing a short and blowing the lights in the house. But there was no short. The passage was even brightly lit, and apparently so was the flat, as they could see even through the closed door, and when they opened it Rutchen was sitting on the floor, her hair pinned around her head, the ends singed. Her sleeves were rolled up and there were little round marks on her arms. There was a dead cigarette in her mouth, and her torso swayed slightly forwards, bending over the flickering pile of charred silver foil and burnt tracing paper that gave off a smell of hot metal. On her knees was her leather purse, gaping and empty, and she was staring with glassy eyes at the flame. Shlezi stood still in the doorway, stunned, and Gerda, alarmed, let out a little shriek. Rutchen raised a puppet hand in a gesture of reassurance. It's nothing, she said, just a bit of small change. Her look was cold with triumph. There's nothing to worry about, she said, it didn't burn. Only the paper did.

Shlezi didn't move. He looked at her fearfully. His face was bloodless and he stood, petrified, hardly comprehending what was in front of his eyes. The air around him was very bright and trembling with bits of the charred silver foil, swarming like little black worms. At the bottom of the pile the coins lay quietly, faded and lusterless. Rutchen went on sitting there, looking alternatively at the two people frozen in the doorway and the dream writhing on the floor. Her face was damp and now two white diamonds were shining in it, and Shlezi looked at her dumbly. A terrible heat ran through him and he went out to the balcony, looking at the illuminated building surrounding him, suddenly understanding that he had never understood anything. For a moment he knew what he wanted to say with a clarity he had never known before. He felt grace, and something new, cool and mysterious, touching his body and enveloping his whole body in a soft robe of silk. He tried to breathe deeply, to fill his body with the touch of the silk, and then he felt his body shrinking, too small for the new understanding. He stood still, too frightened to budge from his place, not remembering what he had understood a moment before. The terrible heat pierced his chest in the direction of his arms and through the bones to the depths of his back, and he felt a terrible pain splitting his back. He moved his head in terror. The head moved, alive. He heard the blood pounding in his neck and he stretched his neck for a minute, feeling the aorta with his fingers, seeing clear pale sky surrounding him like a river. Again he stretched his neck, floating up again, but something in his stomach plunged and he began treading on the spot, already sensing he was treading on nothing. Big cold drops fell onto his eyes and he raised one hand and wiped the sweat from his forehead, stumbling into the room. Rutchen was still sitting there next to the fire and he stood gazing at her in horror, parting his lips to say something but not hearing his voice. He opened and shut his mouth a number of times without managing to say anything, and went on standing, gazing at Rutchen in horror, trying for one more minute to suck his daughter's eyes into himself, feeling her face coming close to him perhaps for the first time, and he clearly saw the black line dividing it down the middle, the birdlike movement and the hostility wiping away any other expression off her face: He clearly saw the crack opening in the floor and the yawning pit. The cold climbed to his neck, his head swayed slightly, and he licked his lips as if he felt a terrible thirst.

The funeral took place a few days later, because it happened on a Thursday and they needed time to get the notices in the paper and let the drivers know, so that there would be drivers at the funeral. On Sunday the cemetery was full up and they couldn't find a good time, so they put it off to Monday, although Gerda didn't like Mondays. Luckily the hospital didn't put any pressure on them, because the refrigerator wasn't full and one more corpse didn't bother them. But the truth is that he had a small funeral, only a few neighbors and a few drivers, who whispered together throughout the ceremony. Mrs. Klein said that he died of sorrow, and Mrs. Borak said it was because he couldn't live without small change and he was afraid to go near it, yes, he was afraid to go near it, she said. One of the drivers said that it was part of the job, you couldn't do without small change, and the man who eulogized him said that it was true, he was a first-class driver, always on time and never short of change, he always had enough small change. He prepared it in advance. He was always prepared. He was very loyal to the job. He understood the job. He understood that driving a bus was no laughing matter, and he loved it, he said, he was the type of person who enjoyed serving others. Mrs. Klein tittered and Mrs. Borak whispered something and Gerda stood without moving, with the plaster cast round her neck making her seem even more mummylike. The sun began sinking early. Weeds grew on the surrounding paths and a wind blowing from the sea shrouded her tall silhouette and its look of a skeleton standing erect looking at the fresh earth. Rutchen too stood very still. She bent down and placed a small stone on the grave. Then she turned around, walking slowly, receding slowly towards the main path and walking along the path, keeping to the side with the light, like a person laboriously crossing a plain. Afterwards she went up to the beggars and pushed the pile of small change she had in her pockets into their tins. Afterwards Gerda's silhouette sat at the window, as on every evening, frozen, and Rutchen stood on the balcony, her sleeves rolled up, looking at her hands, and I saw her cautiously stroking one hand with the other, as if fingering the nonexistent tattoo, perhaps feeling the ink swelling in her veins, slowly but steadily poisoning her blood.

Afterwards she brought her mother food, and from our balcony I saw her bending over Gerda, who was sitting and picking at the green oilcloth with the little pink flowers crumbling on the table like roses.

All evening long they did not exchange a word.

It was a clear night with low stars. The wind changed to a hot wind passing dumbly, without a sound, from the mountain to the balconies in the courtyards below, and the sense of evening came down early on the courtyard which always looked particularly beautiful in the evening, the sinking light enveloping it like a large coat with gigantic sleeves full of resonant air still echoing *earth to earth ashes to ashes dust to dust*. For a moment it seemed that the twilight was permanent and the plunging ball of fire would never sink. The air was full of pensive sweetness. The gigantic sleeves waved madly. Then all at once an ominous darkness descended, Rutchen's nervous giggle was heard and she could be seen bending over her mother saying something in a lowered voice. But Gerda did not move. The beam of light from the opposite window crossed her tall silhouette and from my balcony I saw her back tensed against the back of the chair, as if she were tied to a pillar.

Late at night, when I stepped onto the inner balcony, the tired neighbors were still clustered cosily round Mr. "Everything Cheap"'s table, enclosed in the ring of their own consuming curiosity, and there was still a question hanging in the air, as if someone unknown had been temporarily defeated. Mrs. Klein said that when all was said and done it was a sad story, and Mrs. Borak said that all stories were sad. And let's not forget, she said, that it was an easy death, and that's a blessing, that's definitely a blessing. She seemed to like the sound of the word "blessing" very much, because she repeated it a third time: That's definitely a blessing, she said, and added that they mustn't forget that there was still the small change, too, which was confirmed by "Mr. Everything Cheap," who had more detailed information about the bundles in the closets and the beds and even in the storage space above the bathroom and above the kitchen. He expressed the opinion that it was because of this that the funeral had been postponed, because of the shroud, because they must have wanted to sew deep pockets in the shroud, and he licked his lips, making a little sucking noise when he added that it would take very deep pockets indeed to hold the piles of small change. If it was bank notes, it would have burnt, said Mrs. Klein. Mrs. Borak was silent, and Mr. "Everything Cheap" remarked that he certainly knew what he was about, hoarding that small change, a remark that gave rise to a peculiar hilarity, which he immediately made a conspicuous effort to control out of respect for the dead and the recency of his demise. But the timing turned out to be unlucky, and one week later the currency was changed again. Mr. "Everything Cheap" was the first to hear the news and he hurried to pass it on to Gerda, with the same peculiar hilarity, hinting with exaggerated concern at the stacks of coins in the closets and the storage space, and giggling irrelevantly a little. Gerda didn't answer. She straightened up, as if his voice was reaching her from a long way away. Now too her face was long, smooth and empty, and she thrust her body forward, throwing herself into the air. Late at night she was still staring into the empty street, then into the opposite house, then up into the sky. Mr. "Everything Cheap" heaved a tender, commiserating sigh, and added that they would have to start going to the bank, and Mrs. Klein, with the expression of pensive sweetness on her face, said they would need a bus for it. Back to the bus, she said.

As for Rutchen, they said she shrugged her shoulders, and they said she even breathed a sigh of relief, smiling blandly and not reacting. From my balcony in the evening she could be seen, sitting very still. The bus, as I said before, was no longer standing in the street, and it was a long time since Shlezi sat in the window. But sometimes, in the evenings afterwards, I too saw him, sitting and counting small change. I would say to myself then something I learned a long time ago, that just as life carries in it death so death carries in it life, and that must surely be what Rutchen thought too when she said: You see, he's still sitting in the window, arranging the small change. The two silver tacks inside her eyes burned erratically as she said it, flickering like a failing battery, fluid with invisible tears, repeating fanatically: Every day, arranging the small change. It seemed to me that I could actually hear the sentence, said out loud, like a conversation continued in the next room or behind a tree, as if the words were coming out of her body. Now her face was netted with tiny red veins and it bore an extraordinary resemblance to her father's face, as if there was nothing between them now but the short distance at the end of the road. She covered them with her hands, crushing them slightly. Every day, every day, she said.

Translated by Dalya Bilu

I would often see her walking down the street or sitting on the yellow bench in the park opposite my kitchen window, and she was always wearing a lace dress in the "layered" style that had gone out of fashion long ago, but which hid the holes in the dress, although in the seventies holes were in fashion too, and she was usually holding a white parasol in her hand, and my neighbor sighed nostalgically and said that the parasol reminded her of Tel Aviv when it was small and nice. She had long fair hair arranged in corkscrew curls, carelessly cut, high and low and high and low again, apparently she cut it herself and then muddled up the hair and the corkscrew curls. In summer she wore white canvas shoes embroidered with flowers, in winter the same multilaced boots all winter, and sometimes she would suddenly open the parasol and begin walking quickly as if drawn somewhere by a magic wand, and only rarely did I see her walking slowly, and then she said to me, yes I'm walking on clouds.

This sentence, walking on clouds, I heard from her a number of times, and when I once told her that birds flew through clouds she said: Oh, yes, the seagulls. It was mid-day and it was quite hot and there were no people in the park, and we sat in the shade of a pine with a broad treetop. There were a few clouds which at first seemed heavy, almost threatening, but they quickly scattered, and by mid-day I already knew a few things, although she spoke in a rather confused way and it was a little difficult to understand what came first and what came afterwards, but I understood that it was a matter of love, and these things, of course, are difficult to understand, but after an hour I already knew that she came from Ashkelon and for years she had dreamt of coming to the big city, and when she arrived she was lucky and she got a job as a waitress in a pub, and one night he came into the pub, ordered a beer, and didn't take his eyes off her. He had bulging, starving eyes, which from his corner outside moved over her whole body and devoured her shoulders, her hips, her legs, her breasts, her stomach and her neck, and when she finished her shift he followed her silently, and then he approached and walked next to her without touching her, and without a word followed her into her home, closed the shutters without a word and undressed her slowly without a word.

She received the white parasol from him after the third night, wallowing all night naked in the sand with the waves flooding them and receding and flooding them and receding again, and in the middle of the night she suddenly said to him: Imagine we had a white parasol in the night which made us a little white canopy over the sea, and he said, and you were a bride, and she said, I'm a bride I'm a bride, and the next day he appeared with the white parasol. He said that he had searched all the secondhand shops on Dizengoff Street without finding a white parasol anywhere, and he had already decided to go to the flea market in Jaffa the next day, perhaps there was a white parasol lying around there somewhere, but just then, already exhausted and despairing, he suddenly saw peeping out of the bottom of a pile of shabby old velvet cushions, in a shop right at the very end of Dizengoff Street, the stick of a parasol, and imagine, it was white, he said. When she told me this she smiled a stray smile, as if the smile lay not on her face but outside her face, and afterwards she stood up quickly and walked away, and from the corner of Shaul Hamelekh Boulevard I saw her standing, not crossing even when the traffic lights changed, and only looking at the changing light, waiting for the traffic lights to stop and the street to empty so that she could cross the empty street slowly with her parasol.

It was a white linen parasol, closely woven, like canvas, on a silver-colored metal stick with a little silver-colored handle surrounded by a narrow brass ring, the linen finished in scallops with ruffles of lace, it was apparently a very old parasol, because the years had wreaked havoc on it adding stripes of grey and ochre and even earth-brown, and in the morning she would hang it on a nail on the wall next to her bed, but it was opposite the window and the parasol swayed, and she got a drill from her neighbors and bought a few wall plugs and tied it with long boot laces to screws in the wall plugs so that she could undo the boot laces.

Already on the first morning, when she woke up, the bed next to her was empty and she realized that he had gone, and only then she remembered that she didn't actually know who he was at all, and she smiled to herself. Then she leaned out of bed and looked in the mirror, not believing that it was her, it was her it had happened to, and she got up quickly in a panic and stood naked in front of the mirror. It suddenly seemed to her that it was somebody else in the mirror, and she turned in a panic to the bed. The light from the slits in the shutters wove pale lines on the rumpled sheet and creased pillows and the low iron headrest, and she was afraid to sit on the bed. Her face was cold and she felt her face, leaving her hands there for a long time, feeling the cold passing from her face to her hands, and she rubbed them together and slowly carefully stroked one cheek, then the other, then she passed her hands over her feet, and again she smiled when she remembered how he had kissed her feet, trying to remember if she had been curled up in him or he in her, and she laughed a little. The shutter was still closed. Butterflies of light danced on the bed, casting golden bubbles on her hands and arms, and she saw him looking at her from the end of the pub with his starving eyes, and with these eyes walking slowly behind her, not approaching and not touching and only at every street lamp turning his head with those staring eyes, and with these eyes slowly following her into her home. When she sat down next to the mirror she panicked for a minute to see the raspberry color on her lips, but she immediately said to herself that she must have bitten her lips, and went back to bed. From the closed shutter the butterflies of light danced now on her face, and she uttered a sad little bleat, not knowing if she was floating or falling, and suddenly she saw opposite her something green dazzling and sat up.

After getting dressed she went to the nearby café and ordered hot coffee and a croissant with butter. Then she repeated the order. I'm mixed up, I'm all mixed up, she said to herself and ordered a third cup of coffee. The waiter said: Ho ho, what is the matter with you today? And she said: Why? What's wrong? And the waiter said: Nothing, you're fine, you're just fine. Something pressed on her eyes and she thought again that she knew nothing about him and when she told him that her name was Vardina he laughed and said: Vardinina, and that was almost the only time during the whole night that he laughed, repeating the name Vardinina a few times, and also almost the only word he uttered, and suddenly she thought about the silence. Oh my, what is the matter with you today? repeated the waiter, and she said again: Why? What's wrong? His snigger worried her now, and suddenly she felt something hollow in her whole body. It was already late in the morning. The light was growing yellow, and she went out into the street, roaming restlessly. When she returned the butterflies of light had vanished. The darkness cleared. The sheets were still rumpled, full of the smell of his body, and she bent over the bed, sniffing. Suddenly she started trembling all over her body and remembered that she had trembled like this while making love. God, it happened to me, O God, it actually happened to me, she said, going to the window and opening the shutters, looking at the people walking in the street, not understanding how they could be walking like yesterday and the day before yesterday as if nothing had happened. Someone ran hurrying to catch the bus, a young girl ate an apple, and an old woman who stumbled on a broken paving stone sat down on the curb. In the distance, on the strip of sea at the end of the street, a frame of violet-blue radiance glimmered with the waves a blur inside it. The aluminum balconies opposite her glittered, wrapped in a hot lemon veil, and she stood for a long time at the window, forcefully gripping the rail. She saw the waiter wiping the tables, the old woman getting up and continuing on her way, the girl with the apple disappearing into an entrance of an intercom, and the radiant strip of the sea becoming narrower, almost a narrow cone receding behind some dark glass, and she saw the cuts of light between the buildings, the trees and the water, as if she were seeing them right inside her body. Her head became completely transparent, the sea-cone turned into a big long aquamarine eye and she said: My God, Vardinina, that's what he said, and moistened her lips with the tip of her tongue. Suddenly she started searching the room to see if he had left anything, turned over the pillows, the clothes on the chair, but he hadn't left anything, and she suddenly felt giddy and sat down on the bed. Her hair was damp and she said: I'm sweating, my God, why am I sweating. The Vardinina rang again in her ears and she knew for certain that he would come that evening to the pub, and even though she was in the kitchen at the moment it happened she knew for certain that at that moment he had entered the pub and like yesterday ordered a beer, looked at her with starving eyes without saying a word, and she knew for certain that he would sit and wait until her shift was over, and he waited.

After twenty-three nights—she counted, of course she counted, and then she counted again and then she counted again and then again— when she woke up in the morning, the bed next to her was empty as usual but her heart didn't tell her anything, and this too she repeated to herself afterwards, that her heart didn't tell her anything, not a thing, and for a long time she reminded herself of this. As usual she went downstairs for coffee, ate her croissant spread with butter, drank one cup of coffee and then another, and early in the evening went to the pub. It was a grey day with the first signs of autumn in the air. The wind was dry. On the tables dry leaves blew from the avenue and she swept them away time after time, but even when the night deepened she did not see the starving eyes on his bench. For a moment she panicked when someone sat there, luckily for her the someone left immediately, but later too the starving eyes were not seen. At eleven o'clock at night she was already feeling a slight sourness in her mouth, her body grew heavy, and she broke two empty beer glasses and overturned one full glass of beer. Even after the pub emptied she still looked for something to clean here and something there, collected the rubbish and even went out into the yard to empty it. Afterwards she gulped down two glasses of beer and felt very tired. Her head spun giddily and she dragged her feet slowly home, walking on the side of the pavement where they always walked, expecting him to be lying in wait for her somewhere, afterwards saying to herself that perhaps he was waiting next to the entrance railings. When she opened the door she did not recognize the room even though everything was in its place. The sheet was still rumpled from the morning and also the pillows and the cotton blanket, and the parasol was still on the wall next to the bed, and she lit the lamp, but the bulb was burned out and she began unscrewing it nervously until it broke in her hand. Her fingers were full of blood and she looked for a plaster, forgetting where they were and not finding anything in the dark. Suddenly she remembered that blood was a remedy against danger. When she was still a child her father had told her so, and she began to search nervously, unable to remember where she had put the spare bulbs, opening the kitchen cupboards nervously and forgetting to close them, and the corner of a door jabbed her in the head, but she went on searching without finding a new bulb. When she found one at last and switched on the light she felt a sharp pain in her forehead and saw that she had a bruise there, and she took a knife, wet it and pressed it hard against the bruise, feeling the coldness of the metal penetrating her forehead, and she stood for a moment next to the window. The street was empty. A car alarm sounded a maddening whistle, and again there was silence and she lay down in her clothes on the bed and for a long time she lay there with her eyes open in the dark. Then she got up and opened the shutters. The open shutters illuminated the parasol in a pleasant dimness and she lowered it a little, bringing it right down to her head, her eyes fixed on the white canopy of light. The first thought that came into her head was that perhaps he had been called up for reserve duty in Lebanon or Gaza, and he hadn't said anything because he didn't want to worry her, and she decided that she should go to bed, but instead she went downstairs and walked to the pub. The pub was dark. The benches nailed to the pavement were covered in soft velvety dew and gave off a pleasant dampness, and she sat down for a moment on his regular bench, leaning against the backrest. The wooden board was damp and so was her back. There was a forgotten ashtray on the table and she tapped it and made rings with it on the table. The street looked wide. In the leotard shop stars sparkled and also on the pavement, and she dragged her feet home with a burning face and pursed mouth, closed the door and lay down on the bed, imagining that at any minute he would be standing next to the bed, and from time to time she got up and opened the door, but the corridor was empty and she immediately locked it again, listening for a rustle on the stairs or the sound of footsteps coming down the street, but there were no footsteps. Next to her head the white parasol shone and she saw him in every corner of the room, as if there were an electronic eye hidden there, but the electronic eye quickly disappeared. Her face tightened as if about to burst, and she began prowling very quietly round the room. When she went to the window the sky was a blackening blue, and she saw a sky that seemed piled up into many skies, and remained standing, looking. It seemed to her that there was someone sitting on the fence opposite, and she said: Is there anyone on the fence? But the silence continued. The blue became stained with purple. From the street a coolness blew which felt good on her back, and she remained standing in the purplish blue, pressed against the window railing.

When it started to grow light she went down to the café and glanced nervously through all the newspapers. Everything was all right. Nothing worrying had happened, and she ordered her croissant. When a week had passed it occurred to her that he might be in the Security Services, which would account for his silence, and perhaps he had been sent off suddenly on a secret mission. This thought calmed her and she started the countdown, which never ended.

In the café sat cab drivers talking loudly about the latest fantastic goal, arguing about which player would be crowned footballer of the year, their cigarettes making a mushroom cloud of smoke, and she buried her head in the newspaper. The paper suddenly seemed full of incomprehensible black dots. The close palm in the avenue cast a panther-green shadow on the table. The air showed signs of fine weather which grew increasingly finer. From the end of the street came the sound of a receding siren and afterwards the usual medley of noises. The pasta shop next door opened, and also the shoe shop, and she stared for a moment at the fluorescent bulbs duplicated in the mirror, at the shelves with the new shoes arranged in a row, seeing the walls collapsing and turning into stars, and said to herself that she had to go home but it seemed to her that as in a dream she would arrive at some other place.

Once she told me that in the middle of the night when she went home a motorcycle nearly ran her down. It was on that night, she said. Another time she said that there had apparently been a fire somewhere, because a fire engine was racing so fast that it almost ran her down. It was on that night too, she said. Another time she told me that they were repairing the electricity at that end of Ibn Gvirol Street and there was a pit fenced with barbed wire and a sign, but it was dark and she didn't read the sign and got stuck on the fence, unable to free her dress from the barbed wire that pierced her dress. It's lucky I didn't get electrocuted that night, she said. When she told me this she already had big pale eyes that squinted every now and then at the parasol on the bench, holding one hand on her stomach as if she felt fear that gave her a stomachache.

Sometimes she got a rash on her hands, as if she had been bitten by bloodsucking mosquitoes, or she would suddenly stand up with a sharp movement, hearing a voice or seeing a shadow crossing the park, and then she would try in vain to think about something but she couldn't find anything to think about. Sometimes the air in the room would suddenly fill with quiet electrical discharges. The bubbles of light on the avenue in the window reminded her of the darting green eyes of cats. In the distance the sea retreated. And she said to herself: Let evening come already, let evening come, but when it started to grow dark and they lit the lights—the lamps swayed as if they were broken and she didn't go to work and the next day too she didn't go to work. Everything already seemed then like something that had happened a long time ago or that hadn't happened at all, but then in the mornings she saw him clearly standing in front of the bed, bending over and saying, Vardinina, and she felt that she had a lump in her throat and started coughing loudly. She looked at her watch. It was six o'clock. At this hour the bed had been empty then too, and she looked again at her watch, which didn't move.

. . .

By then she was already spending long hours in bed, especially in the
mornings, listening alertly to the silence in the room, moistening her
lips with the tip of her tongue, sensing how the days were passing in a
different kind of time, which was measured not in hours but in steps,
often leaving the door open in the certainty that he would come in the
middle of the night, or steal into the room before dawn, and for a long
time she was afraid to change the sheet. Once she told me that she
loved sheets with flowers and asked what about me. Plain sheets, I said,
only plain, and she said: if you only knew what sheets with flowers
were like, and I told her that in my childhood I used to sleep on sheets
with flowers. We had narrow iron beds when we lived in Nesher, I told
her, and once I suddenly felt something crawling over the bed. When I
switched on the light there was a black scorpion crawling over the sheet
and my mother screamed, she said that black scorpions were fatal and
she said: What a miracle! She asked me if the black scorpion had stung
me and I didn't know, and what did my mother know. I told her that
we had sheets with flowers then because my mother loved sheets with
flowers and she would buy sheets with red flowers and pink flowers,
and when I was a child I slept on pink flowers. She laughed and said
that maybe my mother wanted the pink flowers to pad our dreams and
lives, and I said, yes, she would wash them twice a week by hand on a
washboard, in those days people still did their washing on a washboard, it was made of hard corrugated tin, but they called it a washboard, and she asked about the scorpion. I told her that my father simply took a hammer and killed the scorpion and then my mother
changed the sheet for a sheet with different flowers, and threw the old
sheet into the laundry basket, but a little black stain remained in the
heart of one of the flowers, and she said that it was forbidden to sleep
on a flower with a black scorpion stain and kept the sheet folded up in
the cupboard. The scorpion was long dead by then, I said to her, and
she asked why anyone should be afraid of a dead scorpion. I said that I
didn't know, I was only a child then, and I told her that we used to hike
to the forbidden caves in Wadi Rushmiyye, and on the stone walls or
the earth walls we found wonderful paintings under the cobwebs, and
we found curses and we found words and we found love paintings, and
she asked what are love paintings. There were huge signs that entry to
the caves was forbidden because of cave fever, I told her, and she asked

if we had fallen ill with cave fever and what this disease was. We were children, I said to her, we were children, and I don't know the secrets of the cave. She asked if we had ever reached the end of the cave. I told her that it was impossible to reach the end of the cave because it was a hole inside a mountain. She asked if this was what was written in the dictionary. I told her that I hadn't looked it up but perhaps this was what was written in the dictionary, and I told her that once people used to put big stones in the mouth of the cave. But I don't know how to put stones in the mouth of the cave, she said and suddenly asked if I had a ladder at home. Yes, I said. She asked what color the ladder was. White, I said. She said that today there are ladders painted red, there was a red wooden ladder, and she wanted to buy a red wooden ladder. I said that a red wooden ladder was nice. But what I've got in my head is a cave, that's what I've got in my head, she said and laughed.

The next day I saw her sitting opposite my kitchen window on the bench, eating a sandwich wrapped in cellophane and not finishing it, but wrapping it up again in the cellophane and returning it to the big velvet bag that was lying next to her on the bench. The white parasol was lying closed next to her, and she sat stooped, leaning on the back of the bench the way one leans on the railing of a bridge, and I remembered the matter of the cave and the cave fever, and how she had said that's what I've got in my head, and laughed. Her face was turned away and I only saw her profile, the treetop casting stripes of shade on it until it looked as if it had been smeared with stripes of iodine. She crossed her legs and seemed calmer, and I thought of the fear and of what came after the fear and hope, like a celluloid film when the gelatine begins to peel off, and I wanted to tell her that there was nothing that forgetting didn't wipe out and memory didn't distort, but I said to myself that our lives were too short to reach this point, and I wanted to tell her something about this but I didn't know how and what. In the meantime I saw her opening the parasol, which suddenly seemed stiff, as if it were made of fiberglass, and the lace trim widened, its contours making ruffled arcs like lace panties, and I remembered her face when she said to me: I have a lot of voices in my head that paralyze my head, and something else that I don't remember. Her raspberry lips tightened in a smile, yes, I've been infected by the virus, she said, and I saw her fingers trembling on the metal stick of the parasol. Afterwards she tapped her nails on the stick so sharply that it sounded like a metal tapping on metal. Her face took on a wild look. I told you, my body remembers it, she said. Afterwards she said that in the morning she had dreamt that she was walking in the street and suddenly her forehead collided with a wall and she woke up screaming. There was something violent in her voice, and she lifted her hair hitting herself with little blows on her forehead and laughed. It's the morning demons, don't you know the morning demons, those that make a half shadow around the shadow, don't you know them? she said. Her face crumpled and she laughed again. Yes, those that make a half shadow around the shadow, you must know them, she said.

I still thought then that she went about with the parasol so that she would be recognized both from a distance and from behind, but afterwards I had other thoughts. It was already winter then and she wore a rough poncho in an off-white color, with checks of ochre-brown and long milk-white tassels, and when it rained the parasol dripped and so did the tassels, the off-white mingling with the milk-white, and when she sat on the bench to rest a permanent light drizzle fell on the parasol from the foliage of the tree, and my neighbor said: Look look how she's sitting there with the rain on her head, but I said to her: No, she has a parasol on her head, and my neighbor smiled. She has birds in her head I'm telling you, that's what she's got in her head I'm telling you, birds making her crazy in the head, I'm telling you, and I said: If you say so I suppose you know what you're talking about. Yes, that's what she's got in her head, my neighbor said and went on watching her from the window, smiling in enjoyment.

When I was a child I once received as a present a little box made of bamboo peel and inside it dolls that ate sorrow. Relatives who had been in Mexico brought it for me from Indians they met on the Mexican border, Indians who would put the box under the pillows of little girls in the night, and at night the dolls would eat the little girls' sorrow. The box was two centimeters wide and three centimeters long, and the tiny dolls were made of wire with exquisite threads of silk wound around them, and they had heads the size of a pin, and for a long time I kept them under my pillow. The box was oval, and when I asked my mother why it wasn't round she said that sorrow was never round, and when I asked why it wasn't square she said that it had no edges, the sorrow. I put it under my pillow every night then, and in the morning I was afraid to open it because even the pillow was full of sorrow. One day when I got up the box was gone, and my mother said that perhaps the sorrow had eaten the box, and then I asked how to close it, the sorrow, and my mother laughed. When I told this to Vardina she said that with her they had eaten the pillow a long time ago, and she too laughed.

At first the longings softened the pain on her face, but that was still in the summer, when she would walk along Frishman Street to the sea, saying that she loved Frishman Street because it had a tunnel of wind from the sea, snatching up some ragged branch on the way or walking barefoot along the beach, leaning against some deserted wall on the way to Jaffa. For the most part it was already evening. The walls were moldy. The canvas parasol looked as transparent as if it had been made of muslin, and she would stand leaning against the wall, looking at the fan opening above her with the lace ruffles. Afterwards I saw her sitting on the bench in the park in Dubnow Street, and after a while she stood up and disappeared again at the end of the street, and like a figure in a Chaplin film turning into a little dot with a black ring closing round swallowing the end of the film.

Sometimes I thought that she was still searching for him in the streets. Sometimes I thought that she had stopped long ago, seeing her lying on the bench, curled up like a ball, pulling the parasol closer to her body, perhaps still hearing his footsteps from the corridor, from the stairs, approaching more and more often, and then receding more and more often, but still standing behind every window and every lantern and only she was in the wrong place and forgot the rules of balance and didn't find the right place.

I'll never know what happened to him, I'll never know what really happened, she said to me that summer. She said this very quietly. It was early in the evening. Distant lines came closer to each other and became one, and afterwards it was quiet and even the noises of the street closed in a single chord, and she stood up and took a few steps in an undefined direction, and turned towards Shaul Hamelekh Boulevard taking measured little steps with her feet close together as if her feet were tied.

Although it was summer she wore short boots of a light-colored leather that her father had bought her, and she wore them in the summer and in the hamsins too, and when I told her that I had once read that there were nations that wore boots with spikes in the soles in order not to kick the earth, so as not to anger the earth, she said: You see, there's hope for me, and smiled her stray smile, suddenly sobbing, and afterwards she cried all evening in all the streets on all the benches in the streets, pressing to her skull the white canvas dome that moved above her like a bodiless rag in the dry summer wind.

The next day she sat in the park, quiet, and when she saw me she said: He's alive, he's here in the street, I just don't know which street.

Later on she said that she had walked right down Dizengoff Street to the old harbor, and when she passed a secondhand shop there was a woman standing there who recognized the parasol. She said that it had been bought in her shop. He said then that he needed a little gift. She understood that he was my husband, she said, and she was surprised that he hadn't come back to look for another little gift. He was so eager, she said, and told me how he had rummaged and searched and turned the whole shop upside down, turned it upside down, simply she said, and how happy he was when he found it, and she asked if he was in town. I told her that he was in town, and she said, yes, I'm glad, and then I told her that he was at home, and I was in a bit of a hurry because he was waiting for me at home, and she said, give him regards from the parasol shop, and she looked at me strangely, you understand. Perhaps she thought something, I said, people think all kinds of things. She gave me a long look. I know them, those looks, I listen all the time, she said. She laughed softly, fingering the lace of the parasol like yesterday. Then she closed her fingers and raised her hands to her temples, wiping one eye with her hand. Her shoulders stuck out, hunched forwards, and I thought that she was probably waiting for me to say something, but I didn't say anything. I took my brief daily walk into the depths of the park. When I returned she was still standing next to her regular cypress, trying to dislodge a bit of bark that had got stuck in the spring of her parasol and looking at me from under the white canvas dome, but now too I didn't say anything, and afterwards I saw her fold the canvas dome and furl the parasol. It was a wet day and it was really cold. A wind blew, whipping the trees, and the parasol swayed, and she held it tight, pressing her eternal little canopy hard to her body. Thick pine needles flew and settled in heaps all over the park and the branches of the cypress tree moved like giant broken hooks unattached to anything, and when I went home I could still hear the whipping wind. Clots of mist were hanging in the air and it was barely possible to see the park, but when I cleared the steam from the windowpane with my hand I saw her, standing pressed against the trunk of the cypress tree, holding the stick of the parasol in both hands. She was just standing there.

That year winter started early, and in October it was already raining. When it cleared briefly fragments of white sunlight were scattered in the puddles on the ground, and she sat a lot on the bench staring at the park that never stopped growing, looking at the buildings opposite. The trees shone and also the crows on the trees, and when the rain stopped the treetops looked like metallic blown glass, and it seemed to her that she knew something with absolute certainty, but she couldn't remember what. When she opened the parasol it seemed to her that one of her arms was longer than the other, and she folded the parasol and laid it on the bench, placed her velvet bag under her head and lay curled up on the bench.

In January there were fine, warm days. Early in the evening the sky dripped gold, and in the middle of winter it already seemed that at any minute spring was about to begin. In the springlike mist even the crows in the park flew full of color, uttering staccato cries, moving above the treetops like underwater plants. Sometimes it suddenly seemed as though a distant storm was approaching, a natural result of unclear meteorological tension, but when it cleared the park looked as riddled and transparent as a net, and with a smile on her face she stepped slowly from tree to tree under what was her umbrella. Her eyes had grown so big that they looked hollow, and she looked as if she were sleepwalking.

In February the rains returned, and when it stopped raining the gutters went on dripping for a long time, and in the evenings she sat a lot at home, switching on the television and switching off the sound, looking at the running pictures, without knowing what was happening on the screen, and during the frequent electricity cuts that year she went on sitting in the dark, looking. Often there was snow on the screen. The snow trembled. Afterwards the television flickered and the picture returned, and she looked at the people moving to and fro and talking. Afterwards she stood up and looked at the grey empty street. The walls opposite looked full of black stains. A solitary light going on across the street shone like a diamond. In the open window the curtains flapped in a cold gust of wind, and she went down to the street, wrapping herself hurriedly in a giant plastic cape so that her body would remain dry and warm, suddenly seeing that she had forgotten the parasol. The night light drew a silver line around the contours of the buildings. The pub was closed, the tables washed, and she sat down. Lightning slanted across half the sky. You could still hear the gutters dripping, and she felt how her head was empty of all thoughts and her memory was completely gone. She hid her face in the plastic cape, as if she had seen a ghost, and ran home in a panic, not understanding why she felt like crying when she found the parasol on the table.

In the middle of winter they transferred her to work behind the bar. The pub was busy all winter. The bar was packed. On the tall stools the people changed all the time, and she poured all the time, her hands moving all the time and also her eyes, lurking like a scorpion behind the counter. On rainy days she took the big yellow plastic cape to wrap herself in on the way home and also the parasol, and she would be very tired when she went home, with bloodshot eyes, and in the pub too, late at night, she would be so tired that the mirrors on the wall flickered shattered and her face was multiplied in broken pieces from every wall. What I look like, she said to herself, fixing her hair and straightening the corkscrew curls, but her head ached and also the roots of her hair, and it seemed to her that her hair was falling out. What will become of me, she said, I don't know what will become of me, and she tied the corkscrew curls into a topknot. Her face suddenly looked different to her, and not recognizing her own silhouette, she said: My face is ruined, my face is simply ruined, rubbing her face and undoing the ribbon and letting her hair fall loose again. It seemed to her that a fresh breeze was blowing through her hair, and she said: I'm tired, I'm simply tired. The mirrors on the wall suddenly grew very large, the pub was all eyes, and through the big windowpane, as in a movie, the street looked like a long corridor with lamps. Suddenly she saw a couple passing, the man walking at a distance behind the woman, and she left the counter, elbowing her way through the crowded tables, and ran outside. But the couple had already receded, crossing the street at a pedestrian crossing. The man's back looked familiar to her and she ran and stood nailed to the spot, looking at them disappearing round the bend in the street. Her head wobbled as if it were about to fall and she leaned against the notice board. No no, she said to herself, it isn't him, I'm already crazy, I'm completely crazy, trying to grasp the spot that was already empty, and she retreated walking backwards, and afterwards she advanced with a zigzag movement, taking a few steps in an undefined direction. Her body was so heavy that it seemed to her she was standing with her whole body, not only her legs. A man sitting alone outside sipped tea and she lingered, looking at him for a moment, turned round quickly and returned to the pub, went up to the tap and drank water. It's not him, it doesn't fit, she said to herself. Afterwards she said to herself: Dammit, what a fool I am. Someone at the bar ordered

III
. . . .
*Fata
Morgana
across the
Street*

whisky, and she said: Right away, right away, hearing her own voice remote and muffled, and went out into the street again and came back and went out again. All kinds of things happen, all kinds of strange things happen, she said to herself, trying to remember what she had seen a moment before but on no account succeeding, and she returned to the bar and poured the whisky. Suddenly it seemed to her that she understood what she had seen before without understanding it, and afterwards she said to herself that she hadn't seen anything and the whole thing was nothing but a mirage, and she repeated this to herself a thousand times. Her legs hurt and she massaged them a bit, to warm up her bones a little. The familiar people in the pub suddenly looked like strangers to her whom she had never seen before, and she went out again to the kitchen, leaned over the tap again and drank water, swallowing in long gulps, and then she straightened up and wiped her chin with her hand. The world's turning, have you heard about it? said the young man who had ordered the whisky and he emptied the glass, ordered another one, leaning towards her over the counter as he emptied the second. Afterwards he set the empty glass down on the counter noisily, seeking her hands, and she quickly lowered them, wiping them on her dress. Listen, life's not so bad, believe me, he said, his whole body already on the counter. His voice sounded familiar to her and she fixed her eyes on him in alarm. Hey, you, what's the matter with you, he said, raised the empty glass ceremoniously and laughed.

I don't know what's the matter with me, I just don't know what's the matter with me, I hear his voice in the voice of every man in the street, every back looks like his back to me, she said to me the next day and smiled gently, lowering her voice as if repainting some pleasant memories, crossing her legs, the stick of the parasol stuck between the paving stones next to the bench, and I noticed that two corners of the parasol had come undone from the spokes and the fabric was hanging limply in the air. She said that last night when she came home there was a strong wind blowing and the parasol had turned inside out, and when she tried to straighten it out again the corners came undone, and I told her that there was a parasol mender on Sheinkin Street, I didn't remember the number. She smiled again gently and said that he had died long ago, picked up the parasol, and examined the fabric that was hanging limply next to the metal spokes. And anyway, there are no more parasol menders in the world, she said.

At the end of winter, while she was strolling down the street in the afternoon, a boy with a Russian accent approached her, holding a gigantic bunch of roses in his hand, and asked her how to get to Katznelson Street. She told him that it was here, on the corner, behind the path between the courtyards, and showed him the path. The boy said that he had been wandering round for an hour and couldn't find the street. Yes, it's a small street, she said, and he held out the bunch of flowers with the name and address on it, apologizing for not being able to read what was written on the note, and she read the name. Her face suddenly flooded with blood, and she read the address slowly, and afterwards went with the boy to the house with the address. My God, I wander round here every day, she said, and the next day early in the morning she was already standing there, and at a quarter to eight she saw him coming out, holding a big black leather briefcase. She waited. Afterwards she walked behind him all the way down Ibn Gvirol Street to the City Garden shopping mall and saw him going into a bank. She waited again, and then went in after him, searching the tellers' counters and recognising his head behind the low glass partition in front of the credit card counter. There was already a queue, and she stood in line. He was no longer wearing the dark glasses he wore then, but only spectacles with thick lenses behind which his pupils looked very small, and she looked at him, searching for the starving eyes, but they were lowered to the pile of papers. She sat down on the bench opposite him in the queue, keeping a tight grip on the parasol, and from moment to moment her hands trembled more. When her turn came she sat down opposite him, hanging onto the parasol with the vestiges of her strength. He asked how he could help her. She did not reply, her hands already trembling on the parasol. How can I help you? He asked again, and she lifted the parasol. He asked again, how can I help you, and she lifted the parasol and placed it on the counter. He asked again, How can I help you? She looked at the folded parasol and gathered the last vestiges of her strength. This is the white parasol, she said. He slowly removed his glasses. Without the glasses his pupils were bigger, his eyes still bulged, but she was still looking for the hunger. He removed his hands from the pile of papers and apparently placed them on his knees. Oh, he said. It seemed to her for a moment that she saw the hunger in his eyes, but he quickly returned his hands to the counter. The shadow of a smile crossed his face. Vardinina, he said. Her whole body trembled at the sound of her name as only he pronounced it, but he asked

113

. . . .

*Fata
Morgana
across the
Street*

again how he could help her. She wanted to say something but her mouth was dry and she couldn't move her tongue, and he said that he was sorry, his wife had gone away then for a month with their child to visit relatives in America, and that morning he had had to go and meet them at the airport. He didn't want to hurt her and therefore he hadn't written her a note to say so, he was sure that it would pass, you know, such things pass, he said. She didn't answer, already clutching the handle of the parasol with both hands. In any case, it was a lovely month, he said. Perhaps he wanted to say something else, but the people on the bench began to grumble and he apologized and said that he would soon be done, it wouldn't take long, and she didn't know why she suddenly opened the parasol and went on sitting there like that, and then she saw that he had put his glasses on again. Behind the glasses there were no longer any irises, but only a motionless white space, and he asked again how he could help her and took hold of the stem of the glasses. I'm sorry, there are people waiting, he said. Someone was already standing impatiently behind her back, and she stood up with the parasol and with the parasol left the bank. In the street she closed it and walked holding it up like that, closed, to the park and lay down on the bench, and through my kitchen window I saw her in the morning lying with the closed parasol, and afterwards I saw her in the same position at noon. An end of winter *hamsin* was blowing. The sun beat down. The shadows were already moving to the other side. A hot wind started blowing the dust in the park and the sand in the sandpit, and she was still lying with the closed parasol, and it seemed to me that she had not changed her position and perhaps she had fallen asleep. In the afternoon, when I made myself coffee, the parasol was still closed, yellow with the sand from the sandpit, and she was still lying in the same position, and I went downstairs. Her face was very quiet, and she said: I saw him, I saw him in the bank, there was a long queue, he didn't have any time. She blinked her eyes, and I thought that perhaps sand had gotten into her eyes, and at first I didn't understand what she had said and afterwards I didn't know what to say. I thought about what had been born in delusion and remained a delusion. I thought: She's still only little more than a child. And I wanted to tell her that there were blind people who remembered the days of light, and something about the long shadow of truth, but she answered me with a staring smile, fixing me with her eyes as if seeking a word she had forgotten but not finding anything. I know, I know, she said. Afterwards she said: And just imagine, he lives here on the corner. Pine needles fell onto her hair and she shook them off. They delivered a big bunch of flowers to his house, perhaps he's had another child, she said, sitting up again. Her voice too was very quiet, and she smiled, leaning back against the back of the bench with her face turned to the street, and I saw only her profile which was so pale that in the strong light it looked almost green.

In the days that came afterwards I still sometimes saw her walking down the street with her parasol furled. As I've already said it was a warm end of winter with days when the *hamsin* blew, but she fought hard against the wind, not letting it blow her parasol away, and one night when I came home late I suddenly saw the parasol opening, and she was standing opposite under a tree, enclosed within the dome of canvas, and afterwards crossed to another tree like a walking lamp among the trees of the park. I hugged the fences, and walked to Shaul Hamelekh Boulevard. When I returned I saw her receding into the depths of the park inside her little private dome of sun, and when I got up to make my first cup of morning coffee I saw her lying on her usual bench in the front of the park, the parasol on the ground, covered with sand and pine needles, the velvet bag open on the bench next to her, spilling a powder compact, two lipsticks, an eyeliner and a little comb, apparently her permanent beauty kit. The white dome was slightly open and also the beautiful curves, the metal spokes glittering in the light like two mandolin strings, and I didn't know if she arrived in the morning or had spent the night there. Since a wind was blowing, the loose fabric flapped, hitting her on the stomach, and I wondered whether to go downstairs, but I remembered how she had smiled gently when she said that there were no longer any parasol menders in the world.

Translated by Dalya Bilu

7. APPLES IN HONEY

. . . .

That summer, I'd go there sometimes, and this week I went again. It was a hot day at the end of summer. A hot wind blew from time to time, stopped suddenly and returned suddenly, full of dust, and when I entered, the place was empty. Not a living soul. I thought of wandering around a bit and then, on the other side behind the shed, I saw the gardener standing and talking with a young woman who sat bent over the stone, moving her head as she spoke, a head wreathed in balls of red curls, glowing like balls of fire in the *hamsin* light.

As I said, the place was empty. The paths had just been swept, sharpening the clean orderly lines of perspective, and in the heavy *hamsin* light it looked more colorful and shining than ever, wrapped in a thin pink coat of fresh watering and new blooming, almost a shining sheath of shining lacquer. And it was very quiet. Not even a sprinkler moved. But as I went along the path everything seemed full of rustling and talking and raspy sounds, rising from both sides of the path from the colored patches of the dense vegetation, as if someone there were grinding glass under the earth.

That was in the most beautiful section, the newly flourishing section of the Lebanon War, which was laden with a rich growth of living flowers and silk flowers and velvet flowers and flowers of thin copper plates and flowers of burlap and flowers of gauze and rust-colored bandages and long serrated cacti with fleshy shoots like explosive caps and tops shaped like an axe.

The woman lifted her face to me.

Do you have somebody here? she asked.

She clasped her knees to her body, didn't take her eyes off me.

I've got somebody here too, she said.

Her knees were really up to her body, and she didn't take her eyes off me.

My husband, she said.

I understand.

Yes, my husband.

I understand.

She turned half her body to me.

My husband, she repeated a third time.

It was quiet. Her eyes were fixed on me, pale, very bright, wide open in dark brown lashes that had nothing to do with the balls of fire, and I don't know, maybe because of the quiet, I said I came here sometimes, hadn't seen her.

Yes, I come once a year, she said. Her voice was low-pitched, almost masculine, almost basso, and she spoke like someone continuing a conversation that had been broken off.

And it usually falls on a hot day like this, a *hamsin*. Always on a hot day like this, a *hamsin*. She banged her knees together, clutched her leather bag to them. And I sit alone. Sometimes with the gardener.

I said I had met him here, the gardener.

She fixed me again with bright, wide-open eyes, raised her hand in the air with a quick movement.

I'm talking to you like I know you, she said.

Maybe we did know each other once.

She laughed, repeating the nervous gesture in the air.

Yes, could be.

Maybe, I said.

She laughed again, covering her knees with both hands. Then she shifted her eyes from her knees and moved closer to me on the stone frame surrounding the small, beautiful garden. She smiled.

He's a good man, the gardener.

The sun apparently blinded her, since she was facing the wrong way, and she closed one eye, and now she looked at me with one eye, round as an animal's eye.

I said: Yes, a good man, the gardener.

She changed eyes, blinking, bent farther over the stone, and opened a cactus coiled up near the stone pillow. Apparently she saw me looking at the date on the pillow. No, No, I come on our anniversary, that's the day I come here, once a year.

Now, too, she spoke slowly, emphasizing every word.

I don't come on any other day. Why should I come any other day?

It was quiet, and even quieter between one word and the next.

And I told you, it always falls on a hot day like this, a *hamsin*. In fact, it was a hot day like this then too, a *hamsin*. She banged her knees together hard, pressed the palms of her hands on them, and said it was impossible to talk about it. I said she didn't have to. She said: I can't talk about it.

You don't have to.

Yes, but when you think.

Better not to think.

That's it, better not to think. That doesn't always work, you understand.

Yes, I understand.

It was quiet. She bent over a bit, leaning forward, unzipped her purse, pulled out a pair of big grey glasses, and put them on.

Believe me, you learn it, and aside from that, time —

I couldn't think of anything else to say.

She zipped up her purse and put it back on the stone.

Yes, time. You believe that time?

I could see her dark lashes drop and open all at once through the big glasses. She took them off a moment and straightened up again, looking around leaning her head back, the way you look out a train window. And in the meantime, everything, almost alive, years, almost alive, she said, turning around to me, and the word *almost* was doubled in the empty garden, hit the air like a pneumatic hammer, and I felt something heavy in my ears and some desire to cover my ears. It seemed to me that was what she did too, but the wind waved her hair, exposing her ears and they suddenly looked small, almost like a little girl's ears. Her eyes moved slowly, wandering over the garden, as if the garden were fleeing behind her, and I thought I should say something but I didn't know what. The light became even lower. The sky a bottomless dome. The blooming roses and chrysanthemums in the beautiful garden burned like scarecrows, and I wanted to tell her that there are many forms of alive, and something about the length of the day and the length of the night, and the simple truth of death and loneliness when that truth comes from the earth and enters your feet and climbs on you through the soles of your feet. Suddenly I remembered the custom that women once used to measure their lovers' graves with strings, and then they folded the strings and doubled them and made wicks of wax candles in honor of their lovers from the wrapped doubled string, and at night, in little cans, they lit the wax candles and all night the long wicks burned in the cans and it was forbidden that the wind should put out the fire in the cans, and I wanted to tell her something about the cans. But she sat quietly, gathering up her hair that was waving from side to side on her neck, moving her fingers slowly through her hair as if the strength had gone out of her hands.

That's it, she said. Her hair was now gathered on the back of her neck and she put her hands back on her knees. In the light you didn't see her eyes, only the lenses of the glasses. She smiled weakly and took off the glasses, closing one eye again as if it were more and more blinded. It really was very hot. The air grew heavy, taking on an ashen color, holding the movement of a hot dry wind that suddenly approached from some unknown gate, covering that clean, well-swept expanse with a cloud of dust. You smelled a thin odor of smoke and resin. Stone tablets looked taut enough to burst. The fresh paths were filled with arteries of lead and the broken sound of broken flutes approached as if it were going into a cave. The woman facing me pressed her hands to her knees as if she wanted to say: Quiet, quiet, but the sound of broken flutes just grew louder, the leaves over the garden plots folded into burned strips of paper, scattering torn petals all around like grains of oats, and I saw the slight trembling of her hands on her knees. Once again she seemed to want to say something, but I didn't hear what, only how she closed both hands on her knees. The sound of broken flutes grew even louder, the light became really low, almost touching, and in the low light the stones suddenly seemed to be moving, waving like curtains, changing that strange architecture of cut-off limbs and turning into a thick dough over the colorful fermentation over the cracks in the earth, contorting the precision of the well-chiseled tablets, and the paths, the markers, the signs at the corners of the paths, the cracks of radiance and the broken screens, and you couldn't identify any stone now. The roses seemed to be plastic, and the grass full of heat worms, and when the wind passed as it had come, the black inscriptions on the stones still ran around in the air a moment and after a moment only the young woman was seen sitting alone, quiet, in the weary garden. Now too her hands were folded on her knees and she sat in silence.

She opened her eyes, looking at me with a special intimacy.

I'm lucky, there's never anybody here on this day, I'm always here alone.

That really is nice, I said.

Yes, it's nice. And I'm always scared they'll come all of a sudden. But you see, God watches over me, until today that hasn't happened, every year I'm here alone, sitting like this, alone.

Her eyes were fixed on me all the time, with that special intimacy that exists only between strangers.

It doesn't bother you that we're talking, she said.

No, of course not, it's nice, I said.

She said: Sometimes, you know—

Yes, of course, I know.

It's that, when you sit there, looking—

Of course, I understand.

She quickly rearranged her clasped hands, and asked if I had to go and I said, No, I've got time. She said: I'm glad. Then she said: Sometimes, you know, you want to talk. The light fell on her face, where two thin serpents of sweat ran down, and she wiped them off with the palm of her hand—Nothing special, just, to talk. She smiled in pain—You know it, and I said certainly, I know. She smiled again in pain—You always think everything happens to other people. Even when it happens to you, it's like it happened to other people. Her face now rested between the palms of her hands and she lifted it a little, turning aside. Some noise was heard and stones rolling around as in an execution by stoning, and she straightened up, looked, and took off her glasses a moment, putting them back on immediately, shifting them as if she couldn't put them on right. She had long beautiful mocha-colored hands, and I looked at her hands which were circled with wide copper bracelets and rings, a ring on every finger, sometimes two, and when she lifted her arms, the bracelets dropped toward her elbow, linked together making a plate of thin copper. She smiled, bringing the bracelets close to her wrists while looking at me through the sparkling lenses. Then she bent over and took out a blue Hebron glass pitcher, put it next to the stone pillow, and said something about the glass and asked if it was beautiful, and I said to her it was very beautiful. Then she said she wanted to bring velvet flowers because she liked very much to make velvet flowers, especially since fresh flowers would fade tomorrow and she only came once a year, and I said yes, that's how it is. She said: Yes, that's how it is, and stopped a moment, once again moving the glasses that gleamed like two tin tablets. What can you do, that's how it is, she repeated. Her eyes lit up with a strange passion and she shook her head, passed her hand over her throat, and once again I looked at her hands and at the bracelets, which with every movement changed their position, making a dull noise of copper striking. They were very beautiful bracelets, and I noticed that every bracelet was set with different stones, and there was a bracelet with yellow amber and a bracelet with red amber and a bracelet with turquoise and a bracelet with small blue lapis and a bracelet with pink coral stones, as if she had a collection of bracelets on her arms. She said: Yesterday I almost made baked apples, every year I want to do that and I don't, baked apples. She laughed a little—That's what we used to do every year on this day, baked apples. Her voice was parched a moment, and I said that was really good, baked apples. She said: With raisins and nuts, you know that, and I said it was really good with raisins and nuts. She said: And cinnamon, of course cinnamon, and you burn the sugar a little, it's very good when you burn the sugar. She moved away a bit on the stone. We didn't put in honey, but he called it apples in honey, she said. She spoke very quietly now, the shaded dark lashes grew wet from one word to the next, and I said I also make that sometimes, especially at the end of summer. She asked why at the end of summer. Her face grew tense, firm, and I didn't know why I had said that or why at the end of summer, and I felt I had to say something and I didn't know what, and I said it was best to make it with Grand Alexanders, and that I always looked for Grand Alexanders. She listened quietly, and I said it was good to peel a thin strip around the apple so it wouldn't burst when it was baking. Now too she listened quietly. Once again her hair was undone and waved from side to side, and she pressed it, clasping it to her scalp, then she stuck her hand in her hair and wound the ends around her finger.

It's really hot, she said.

Her face was wet and she wiped it with the palm of her hand, moving her hand from her forehead to her throat a few times, then she put her hands down on the surface of the little garden and wiped them with leaves. Her head swayed a bit and for a moment she seemed to be dozing, and I thought about the plants that hoard water in their stems, producing giant thorns for defense. Suddenly I remembered a friend of mine who wanted to be buried under his café under his table, and they told him: It must be somewhere else. And he said: How can I be somewhere else? Under my table, he said, under the table, and even broken up it's all right even taken apart it's all right even with one leg it's all right, and I looked at that strange cemetery, at the stone pillars and the beautiful gardens. Within the emptiness the black letters and the white spaces ran around, moving within air pockets, and that's how she sat too. Her hair still moved from side to side and she pressed it to the back of her neck, then she leaned over, hastily opened her bag and hastily closed it again right away, and seemed to take some hairpins out of it, because she started sticking pins in her hair. It took her time to do it because the curls kept opening up again and fell on her throat, and maybe the pins weren't strong enough to hold the burden of her hair, and she plucked off a branch, smelled it, and then stuck it in her hair, then plucked another one and held it close to me. It had the sweet rotten smell of soft wood and she stroked her face lightly with it, and I said she had beautiful hair and beautiful hands. She laughed a little: The bracelets, you mean the bracelets, and I said the bracelets really were very beautiful. She moved away a bit on the stone—Yes, every year, he would bring me a bracelet, that was his anniversary present. Her bass voice suddenly broke like a watch that falls to the ground, and she straightened up and stretched her back—But I don't wear them, only when I come here. She stopped, rotated her wrist—He loved it when I had bracelets on my hands, so when I come here—her eyes became big, yellow, an owl's eyes, unmoving, and I saw her taking out the bracelets at night and putting them on the table and arranging them in order, and in the morning putting them on in order, and looking at her arms and some bracelets are missing on her arms, and she moves them and counts the missing bracelets.

Her throat was taut and she sat, looking straight ahead.

This is from the first year, she said, pointing to the bracelet near her wrist, the one with the big yellow amber stone that her hand stroked a few times, and I understood that they were put on in the sequence of the years, and the second year he bought her the red amber, and then the turquoise, and then the lapis, and then the coral, and I tried to guess what he would have bought her the year after. Her face was still impassive and you saw only the eyes, and it occurred to me that that was what she was thinking now too and that was certainly what she did this morning and how she went to the mirror, standing, looking, and the amber and the turquoise stones, the blue lapis beads and the pink coral return in the mirror, and she doesn't get the dates right, or the years, and she counts the years, and suddenly I didn't see her but only the bracelets shriveling, narrow, thin, closing on her like handcuffs.

She turned around to me now, making a noise that sounded like laughter, but wasn't.

Usually my arms are empty, I told you, all year long I walk around with empty arms, she said. She laughed briefly again, and I said she really had beautiful arms and they were beautiful even without the bracelets, and I tried to imagine how they looked without the bracelets but I simply couldn't. The copper stabbed my eyes like needles and I felt a slight pain in my eyes, and I didn't even see her arms but only how the bracelets wrapped one of her arms, then the other, and her shoulders her stomach her chest, and she was sitting all wrapped as in a giant rack. No, no, I said to myself, it's the quiet, very quiet, it's a strong light, it's the strong light, how they sparkle, the bracelets, in the strong light, and how she's dressed up for him, living or dead she dressed up for him, what a beautiful dress she put on for him, maybe she even washed her hair for him, its shine is so fresh, and how it waves, burning on her head, making a living crown on her head. She said: I don't wear the rings either, not the rings either, and I tried to imagine her fingers without the rings. She had mother-of-pearl-colored polish on her fingernails and I saw how delicate her fingernails looked. Suddenly I remembered the story of the apples in honey and the small annual celebration. She said: For our tenth anniversary he said he would bring me one with garnets, and I tried to guess when the tenth anniversary should have been, and what he would have bought on the ninth, the eighth, the seventh, but the needles stabbed my eyes, the amber got mixed up with the turquoise, the lapis with the coral, and I said to myself: No no, so much light, you can't sit in such light, I said to myself that was what she was doing now too, the tenth, the ninth, the eighth, and like me she was counting backward and the count was short, and she was saying it will get longer, every year it will get longer, the bracelets will get short and the counting will get longer, and then the arms will get shorter too. But she sat quietly, playing with the bracelets that made the banging sound of copper and a dull ding dong ding dong and I thought I might have met her once in the street at the corner and hadn't recognized her, she had empty arms and I hadn't recognized her, and I said to myself: No no, not that, it's not her, it's the light, impossible in such a light, and it's a mistake, it's all a mistake, but the bracelets were already running around in the garden mixing with the fresh beautiful blossoming, with the black letters and the white spaces and the rings too, and suddenly I remembered empty of all body and his house empty and empty his soul and his prayer returning empty, I remembered don't leave me emptyhanded, oh don't leave me empty don't come empty, and I said no no, the air shrivels and we walk empty, why did I remember that? Where did I hear that? Many years had gone by since I heard that, we stand poor and empty, I heard that, I was a little girl when I heard that, it was always in summer when my mother would murmur that, and our hut was across from the Muslim cemetery and the windows were open and I was afraid of the cemetery, and I said let's close the windows, but she said, it's not the open windows, it's the bell, it's empty, it rings empty.

Something wrong? said the woman. She was playing again with the branch in her hand, and I said I was tired and it was late and I had to go. She smiled. Of course, of course, and if you come next year you'll find me here. She sounded very quiet, almost calm, and I said I would remember the date and come, certainly I would come. Since she didn't answer, I said it really was a very hot day and that wind, and I wanted to go in the evening but I was afraid it was closed in the evening.

She went on playing with the branch in her hand, passing it over her face.

They don't close a cemetery, she said.

When I left, I saw the gardener arranging his tools in the shed, lining up the hoes and the spades, the spare faucets, and a heap of new seedlings. He smiled when I asked about her. Come next year, he said, she'll be here. He locked his shed— She always comes this time, every year, he said.

Translated by Barbara Harshav

e were walking, the two of us, on the prome-
nade when somebody called out her name.
Carmella turned her head around but turned it
back at once, and then somebody called out
her name again. She turned her head around
again and looked a moment, searching, then she turned it back and we
went on walking, but the unfamiliar voice again called out her name,
very close now, right behind our backs, and even before she turned her
head, a man stood in front of us smiling a little.

You don't recognize me, he said.

Carmella looked at him with a thoroughly vague look, and again he
smiled. He had a slightly crooked mouth and his smile rose up on one
side. You don't recognize me, he repeated.

Carmella was still looking at him with that same vague look and she
almost went on walking, but the man stood still in front of us stubbornly with a smile crossing half his face. You don't recognize me? I'm
your husband, he said. The smile spread up toward his forehead, rising
a little more in one direction. That is I was your husband, he said.

Oh, said Carmella. Now it was she who smiled in embarrassment.
Really, she said. He was holding a heavy keyring, playing with it, jiggling it. I recognized you from far away, from the back, he said.

Carmella mumbled something, then she made some apology, but he
stood still, stubbornly. You really don't recognize me? he repeated
stubbornly.

Carmella didn't answer, just looked at him in a slightly odd way.
Underneath her sunglasses I could see that she narrowed her eyes a little and his smile also narrowed a little. I've changed, eh? he said.

Yes, many years, said Carmella.

And you haven't seen me all those years.

Carmella was still looking at him in that odd way and smiling a
smile I don't know how to describe, the sort of smiles you don't know
how to describe, and all the time the man was looking at her, really

devouring her with his eyes. But I did see you, a lot, he said. He laughed now, a little too loud, and Carmella took a step back. Again she smiled that smile I don't know how to describe.

What? she said.

The man went on playing with his keyring, blocking her with his body, his shoulders bending forward, moving along with the keyring that made the familiar jingle. In his other hand, he rummaged in his pocket as if he had some little pocket animal there. Yes, I saw you, a lot. You don't believe it, eh? he said. He had lustful little brown eyes that scampered from her face to her body and back again. Always, whenever I got close I thought you wouldn't recognize me if I approached, but now you looked right into my face. He paused slightly. And you didn't recognize me, he said.

She really did look right into his face now too, but still with that same vague and slightly odd look I don't know how to describe.

He giggled. That's it, so, can I invite you ladies for a coffee? he said and waved his hand in a kind of salute to the nearby café. He did that with the hand he took out of the pocket, then he passed that hand over his face, and went on playing with the keyring in the other hand. Then he said that she hadn't even introduced me to him, and she introduced me, and he said, very nice to meet you, and I also said very nice to meet you, and he said: I hope you don't object to drinking coffee with me. Since he was talking to me now, I said: Why not? There's a nice wind from the sea. Yes, there's a nice wind here from the sea, he said and his eyes moved, both of them, to one side, and it seemed to me that I had already seen him before, although I knew clearly that I had never seen him, but in an odd way, I realized that he had walked behind us rather often when we walked here for the pleasant wind from the sea, which we had done rather often, but that was just a wild assumption, and I remembered only that Carmella really had once told me that before she married Itamar, she had had a short stormy marriage with a man she even didn't mention by name, and she never referred to that again, and to tell the truth, I didn't ask anything else, as if it had never been, but he was standing there, all the time jiggling the keyring in one hand. By then, Itamar had been dead for years, and Carmella had been alone for years, but even alone she didn't mention that short stormy year. I tried to recall what else she said about him back then, but I couldn't recall anything except that she said he looked like Marlon Brando, and she emphasized that a few times, believe me, just like Marlon Brando, and

I stood still and looked at the man who once looked like Marlon Brando. Carmella looked too. He bowed his head slightly, blinked and once again passed his empty hand over his eyes, as if he didn't believe that his hour had really come, the hour he had apparently been waiting for a long time as if he were waiting for his best hour, but that too was certainly only a wild assumption. He had smooth, slicked gray hair and a strip of it fell on his forehead, and he raised it, smoothed it back toward the center of his skull, covering the piece of skin where drops of sweat were glimmering. Again he pointed to the nearby café. The chairs here are comfortable, shall we sit here? he said and again made the same solemn gesture.

Carmella was still hesitating, but he insisted, aware that the shock of surprise had worn off. There's really a wonderful little café here, he said. There really was a wonderful little café there that was almost empty, and he himself cleared a table for us in the middle and held our chairs, and added one empty chair and said smiling: I remember that you like to put your purse on an empty chair, so here, this is for the purse, please. He had an especially pleasant voice, and he pointed again at the empty chair: Here, for the purse, please. Carmella laughed and he said: Thank God you laugh a little, and he moved the empty chair close to her. And you still shlep gigantic purses, he said, and then he asked if that didn't tear her shoulders. She asked what tears the shoulders. The purses, the purses, he said, I never understood what you shlep in the purses. He giggled and again his mouth rose to one side. There are women who seem to shlep their whole life in the purses. He stretched back slightly. I'm starting to talk nonsense, eh? So what shall we order, a small espresso? he said, now playing with the keyring on the table, and Carmella said: One might think you had a palace. Absolutely, I do have a palace, he said, so, shall we start as usual with a small espresso? Now too he looked at her with that look that was concentrated and scattered at one and the same time, that familiar look when you want to rewrite something and erase it at one and the same time, but his eyes sparkled and clearly nothing was erased.

He was a well-preserved man, almost unwrinkled, but there was something nervous in the way his mouth moved, as if the burden of all the years and what he had gone through over the years was concentrated there. And he had a thick neck and his head on top of it looked smaller than it really was, but he had beautiful hands and he played them up when he waved his hand, trying to catch the attention of the waiter who was still rapt in his newspaper, all the while brandishing his pen and apparently doing the crossword puzzle. Carmella really did order a small espresso, and I also ordered one, and he ordered beer. He said that in summer he liked to drink beer. The waiter asked which. Goldstar, he said. The waiter asked if he wanted a small one. No, a double, he said.

It was late afternoon. There weren't many people on the beach and the café, as I said, was almost empty, too, the only ones there were a woman with a Doberman at a nearby table and behind her a girl smoking, and then a man came in with a cello, and next to me sat a couple leaning over the table as if they were deep in conversation even though they didn't say a thing, and as I said, we were facing the sea, which was blue and barely moving with hidden veins of gold. The air was so clear you could see the smallest waves breaking fast, covered for a moment with the glow of fire and for a moment with a flash of water, and a light foam rose and fell like big lace roses. The man put his sunglasses on the table and played with them with one hand and with the other hand he held the glass that was empty now. He asked Carmella how she was and she said fine, everything's fine. He asked how she was getting along. And she said: You see, I'm getting along. He said: I understand you had a good marriage, I had a good marriage too, and she said she was happy. I understand that you went through some hard times, he said, and Carmella said: What can you do, there's nothing to do against life. I understand it's been years, ten years I think, he said. Carmella asked what ten years. I mean that he's been dead, that's what I meant, he said. He shook the empty glass. I was even at his funeral, I stood very close, but you didn't see me, he said. He bent forward a little, didn't take his eyes off her. I saw them lower him into the ground, believe me, my heart ached, he said. His voice became even nicer, almost caressing. That's the truth, my heart ached, he repeated. Then he asked if they had done an autopsy. Carmella asked why an autopsy. So they'd know why, he said. Carmella asked what why. Why he died, he said.

Carmella didn't answer and I of course don't know what she was thinking. He said: You must know that, if they don't do an autopsy on the body, death remains a mystery. His eyes slid slightly aside. What I meant, I meant that so it's a riddle.

Carmella also raised her head now slightly. And now too of course I didn't know what she was thinking.

At that time, I was finishing my residency, he said, and then I decided to be a pathologist. He said it was a very interesting profession, pathology. People didn't understand that. You learn a great deal about a person from the body. His neck was slightly red from the beer and the head really looked small on it now. A very interesting profession, he said. But just then something happened to him. Just then his friend drowned. In fact, he walked into the sea. Can you imagine a person walking into the sea? It took a few days to find the body. She couldn't imagine the body of a drowned man, he said. The sun seemed to blind him, and he moved back a little to correct his point of view. And then he decided to be just a plain doctor, that is, an internist, he said. The sun still seemed to be blinding him because he closed one eye, and the other was open in a strange way, or in fact, half open, like the eye of a carnivorous cat or a dreaming man. He seemed to be waiting for Carmella to say something, but that didn't happen, and again he thrust his hand in his pocket shaking it there as if he had a little pocket animal there. You'd always tell me about Virginia Woolf, remember? he said. You said she put stones in her pockets when she went into the water, and it must have been very cold, the water. Once you said that maybe she wanted to take out the stones but she didn't have hands, her hands then were also stones, you said. You don't remember that? But here the water's warm, he said. He passed one hand over the other and stroked the hand, going back and forth over the fingernails. I noticed that he also had beautiful fingernails and he stroked them with pleasure. Then he bent toward Carmella with a very slight movement as if he were sliding in soft sand. And your sister, how is your sister? Still so lovely? he said.

Fine, she's fine, Carmella said.

The waiter at the bar was nervously chomping on his ballpoint pen. He turned down the radio and said maybe they could help him. He wasn't doing well here, he said. He asked what word meant wisdom that started with the letter S.

The woman with the Doberman laughed. She said: What a great sentence, that starts with the letter S.

The waiter chomped his ballpoint some more.

Starts with S, starts with S, he said.

The woman with the Doberman said: Simple. Sagacity. She blew a smile at the waiter and then leaned over and patted the Doberman's back. Even for a crossword puzzle it doesn't hurt to have a little sagacity, she said.

Exactly, fits exactly, said the waiter. He bent over and carefully filled in the empty squares. Now they want something sweet that starts with P and ends with G. He counted in a whisper. Seven letters, that's it, he said, and something sweet, something sweet, starts with P and ends with G, he repeated, slightly desperate. He examined the newspaper in front of him. And seven letters, need seven letters, he called to the woman with the Doberman.

The woman with the Doberman went on patting the Doberman's back. I think, pudding, she said. She asked if the letters fit.

Wait a minute, wait a minute, exactly, said the waiter. He laughed. Honest, there's electricity in the air, honest, really perfect. He carefully filled in the letters. I tell you there's electricity in the air, he repeated.

The woman with the Doberman asked what about her dinner.

The dinner's on the way, said the waiter. He asked what is common to table and earth. That's what I need now, he said.

Salt, said the man with the cello.

Honest, salt, said the waiter.

The man, who had meanwhile introduced himself as Dov, gulped down his beer. He said that that crossword puzzle was a wonderful thing. He laughed with one eye still half open or maybe half closed. The woman with the Doberman asked again what about her dinner.

Coming, coming, the dinner's on the way, repeated the waiter.

Dov moved his head. In his face, his eyes were scampering all the while, and even though the face was still, there was something deranged in his eyes. They seemed to be passionately waiting for some prey.

The waiter announced again that the dinner was on the way.

Dov smiled, narrowed his eyes. He asked if we wanted something to eat and Carmella said no, thanks, and I also said no, thanks. He said: Shrimps, maybe some shrimps, they're excellent here, the shrimps. Carmella said: You know I don't eat shrimps. I forgot, he said, I beg your pardon, I forgot you don't eat anything from the sea. He laughed. Only what's from the living, he said, meat, as raw as can be. His laugh spread over his face. Steaks, he said, with the blood, there's always a little blood left on the plate, you always gorged yourself on that lustfully.

I looked at him. Carmella looked too.

The man with the cello ordered white wine. Two glasses, together, he said.

Dov moved his head again. And your sister still has the guitar? he said.

Carmella said she had stopped playing long ago.

Dov was still smiling, narrowing his eyes. His nose shook a little, as if it were cut off from his mouth. Is she still so lovely? I forgot, I already asked that, he said. I noticed that one of his eyes again became a little higher. She loved shirts with shoulder straps. When she'd wear shirts with shoulder straps, one strap would fall off, it wasn't hard to bring down the other one. His smile was slightly twisted. Or am I wrong, she didn't wear shirts with shoulder straps? He turned the half of his face that wasn't smiling anymore now, and although he sat forward, he spoke as if it came from behind, and Carmella looked at him oddly. Again I tried to guess what she was thinking. The waiter announced again: I'm stuck, dammit, I'm stuck again, I swear, you got to fill in what is where you turn. Again he sucked his pen. That's a word I won't find, I won't solve the crossword puzzle because of that crappy word.

The man with the cello finished his wine. He said: I'm trying to guess. Pain? Air? Traffic light? Death? His face flushed slightly. He said: Where you turn? That's where, isn't it? he said, bending over and adjusting the zipper of the cello case. Honest, everybody's too busy with his own affairs. It wasn't clear who he was talking to and he seemed to be talking into the cello. I swear, the crossword puzzle is the national sport, he said, still bent over the cello.

The woman with the Doberman shifted on her chair. Once, when the Doberman ran away from me, she said, but the man stopped her in the middle. Don't let him get near the cello, he said, he'll eat my cello case.

You don't have anything to be afraid of, said the woman.

The man thrust his cello between his legs. Keep him away, I tell you, he'll eat my cello case. There was terror on his face.

The girl sitting alone behind him, smoking, woke up. Yes, in Savion, a Doberman ate a person's foot. She took a drag of her cigarette. It was in all the papers, he just ate his foot, she said.

Nonsense, said the woman with the Doberman. She said that yesterday she saw on television that they opened a hotel for cats in Tel Aviv. They get pieces of cooked chicken and canned food there and they bring them objects from home, all kinds of things from home, bring them a blanket from home, toys from home, so they'll feel like they're at home. She pulled the Doberman's leash. And what names they've got, Shendi, Dina, Diana, Louisa, amusing, isn't it? Her face beamed. Really got to help cats in this country, cats are part of this country, she said.

About the foot, said the smoking girl.

Newspaper stories, said the woman.

Dov laughed. Speaking of newspaper stories, he said, I read yesterday in one of the papers that some elements in the tourist department prompted the administration of the morgue in Los Angeles to open a "souvenir" shop and all the profits go to the war against drunk driving, and in that souvenir shop they call "Skeletons in the Closet," they sell finger tags to identify bodies, and bags shaped like a skeleton, and beach towels with skeletons and a chalk marking of the body and t-shirts and mugs, and their motto is: Bodies and death are our business, we're only trying to profit from it, everything costs four dollars including an in-depth tour of the morgue, and the catalogue says: This is the real thing. Honest, that's what the catalogue says. He laughed again.

You understand, and I wanted to be a pathologist, he said.

The smoking girl apparently didn't hear. About the foot, she repeated.

I'm telling you, keep him away, keep him away, the man with the cello repeated in a panic.

The woman smiled a meaningful smile. Dogs don't eat human beings, only human beings eat one another, she said, her face beaming with her philosophy of life, and she gently patted the Doberman's back, whispering something more about human beings. Believe me, he's an excellent friend, she said.

I'm telling you, keep him away, the man with the cello almost shouted. He stroked the cello case nervously.

The silent couple sitting behind us suddenly started talking aloud, in the almost nerve-racking way that somebody talks to you aloud behind your back. I don't understand you, just don't understand you, said the man, and the woman said: But what are you thinking about? I'd like to know what you're thinking about. The man said: But what do you want, I don't know what you want, and the woman said: Nothing, I want nothing. But I hear talk, I hear talk all the time, said the man. Lifeboats, you hear, lifeboats, that's what you hear, said the woman. She laughed a short snort, and for a moment there was silence, then the man moved his chair noisily and his voice became even louder. Really, a lifeboat, maybe there's a lifeboat here, he said. The woman laughed her short snort again and again there was silence for a moment. Yes, a lifeboat, that's what we need, a lifeboat, she said after a silence. The man with the cello turned his head, bent over the cello as if he were

132
· · · · · · · ·
SMALL
CHANGE

enveloping it with his body. I bought a leather case, the cello really loves a leather case. He stroked it with both hands. A leather case is good for it, he said. Because he was talking to me now, I said that a leather case must be good. Yes, he said, it protects the cello. He laughed with delight. Honest, even the cello needs protection, he said.

At our table there was now a silence and I just sat and looked at the sea. I noticed that Carmella was also looking, concentrated on one spot as if she were truly looking into the sea, that at the end of it some gate seemed to be opened wide and something was seen there, as if some solitary white figure stood in the gate, but I said to myself, nonsense, there's nothing on the sea nothing at the end of the sea that went on moving like a living moving creature, holding in it some enormous bright spot expanding and contracting and expanding and contracting again, and it seemed to me that I heard some bells ringing in the sea. Maybe the man with the cello also heard, because he smiled at me. Someone who truly loves my music will never know sadness anymore, said Beethoven. Since I didn't hear I asked what Beethoven said. What I told you, he said, his head toward the lengthening light, raised above the cello, and his face also toward the sea that was suddenly covered with a gigantic cloak, which was a white cloak for a moment and a red cloak for a moment, and suddenly a wind blew the cloak. He turned his head to me. When the music stops where does it go, he said, closing the zipper of the cello case.

Meanwhile the wind reached us and blew Carmella's hair as she sat at the window and Dov looked at her with great concentration. It's good here, beautiful here, he said. Carmella gathered up her hair. Yes, a nice place, she said. She looked distracted, but he went on looking at her with great concentration, playing with his hands in the empty pocket. You don't have to be embarrassed, he said, and Carmella said she wasn't embarrassed. You forgot, he said. Carmella said she didn't forget. No, no, people forget, he said, and he said: Yes, the years ran away, and Carmella said: Yes, time runs away. And I brought you a modest gift, he said. His face became narrow, almost lean, with the two eyes peeping in two flashing narrow crevices, and he rummaged lustfully in his shirt pocket. He said: You must remember the note. Carmella asked what note. The note, that night when you left me, when you left, he said.

Carmella scrunched her shoulders as if somebody had smacked her on her shoulders. I'm asking you, she said, but he smiled with open pleasure—Why? I've kept it for years, to give you a modest gift, and he smiled with even more open pleasure. Honest, I've kept it for years, it's lovely, the note, just a modest gift, and he took out some smoothed and wrinkled note, the kind of papers that show they've been felt by a hand many times, and he slowly spread it on the table, but Carmella didn't look and he slowly folded the smoothed paper fold after fold and put it into the shirt pocket, carefully passed his hand over the pocket, smoothing it through the cloth. He had buttons on the breast pockets that were open, and a flap too, and he raised the flap, drew out the note, and put it in the other pocket, then he took it out of the other pocket, slid it in a straight line in the air between the two pockets like someone passing a straight line in the air between two points that don't meet and put it back in the first pocket. In fact, I could tear it up now and put it in the ashtray, he said but he left it in the pocket, smoothed it again with his hand, as if he were leaving there some open hope.

That note, to this day I take my hat off to you, he said. He smiled again with pleasure. I forgot, I don't have a hat. Somebody apparently launched a kite that suddenly spun around above us like a crazy butterfly, and he waved his hand again in a salute, looking again at Carmella with great concentration, as he played with the button of the pocket drumming on it with one finger. That's it, that's the story of the note, he said in a particularly friendly voice. His voice became even friendlier. But we were talking about something else, we were talking about what? And he closed the flap of the pocket, letting his hand linger there.

There was silence. The couple who were talking aloud before also sat silent, each one leaning on his chair, slightly far from the table, the way people talk without saying a word, and I looked for a moment at the woman. It seemed to me that she said: It's you and not exactly you, and it seemed to me that he said: Should go, don't you think we should go. But they sat, each of them leaning on his chair, as if they were leaning on two far-apart tables. Her lips were gray and I thought she should color them, but she didn't color them and there was still silence, but all the time I seemed to hear it's you and not exactly you, and then their voices truly came to me, again slightly too loud, and the scenario was repeated. The woman said: But what are you thinking about, what are you thinking about, and the man said: What do you want, I don't know what you want. Then the woman said: But you have to understand that, and he said: Understand what? But now the woman didn't answer and only the man with the cello moved his chair noisily. I've got to go, I hate to be late and I'm always late, he said, but he didn't get up.

The big glass pane of the café window was lighted crimson now and facing the horizon the sea looked like a kind of tunnel, and a woman who walked bent over a walker, stepping slowly on the sidewalk clutching the window pane, looked sunk inside the tunnel. Dov changed his posture. I used to go to your plays, he said, his voice became friendlier and friendlier as he went on talking, and he said what plays, and what roles he liked, and even what dialogues were his favorites. He's got a good wife who understood that, he said, and it doesn't bother her that they went together to see her, Carmella, he wouldn't have gone if it bothered her, he asked her about that before every play, was always strict about that, he said, and she said absolutely, it absolutely didn't bother her, and Carmella said: Yes, you told me you've got a good wife. Yes, she even dressed especially for every play, he said, she really cared how she dressed for the play. Once, when we went to a premiere, she even made herself a dress especially for the premiere. As for him, he didn't dress specially, she knows, she remembers, doesn't she? She doesn't remember? Anyway, she certainly didn't see him, you don't see the audience from the stage. He laughed in an especially friendly voice. I was usually your last applauder in the audience. You always curtsy beautifully, he said, he bowed slightly and bent over on the table, moving his empty beer glass so it wouldn't tip over. I almost turned over the glass, he said, why did I move it? Either way, it won't spill, it's empty. His laugh became slightly embarrassing, and Carmella said that when they had been together, he didn't go to her plays. Of course, of course, he said, and again asked about her sister. Then he said again: I forgot, I already asked that. She had such a soft body, I simply couldn't forget how soft her body was. He bent over the table again a little. Her skin, you remember her skin, even in the dark it had a sheen, her skin. His smile rose again to one side. When you had long plays, when she was living with us, he said slowly in a particularly friendly voice, not finishing the sentence and looking at Carmella from the side as if he was not seeing her, the friendly voice becoming friendlier and friendlier with every word. When you played in *Long Day's Journey into Night,* a long play—

Carmella slowly moved her chair aside. It's starting to get cold, she said.

You'd come back late when you played in *Long Day's Journey into Night.*

Your glass is falling on you, Carmella said.

And then, when your sister—it really was a long journey into night, he said. His face was now festive, almost glowing, and he put both his hands on the table. A little cheese? A little sausage? he said.

Carmella looked as if she didn't hear.

And that was a hit, the long journey into night. I forgot, how many times did you play that? You had a good role, he said.

Carmella didn't answer.

And it was winter, heavy rain, and once, when you forgot your umbrella at the theater, when I dried your shoes on the stove, the brown little suede shoes you loved—

Carmella didn't answer.

You were soaked to the skin when you came home from the theater, you shook all night, he said.

Carmella didn't answer now either.

That was a white canvas umbrella we once bought in Paris, on our honeymoon week in Paris, and you said it reminded you of a parasol. You remember it? You don't remember it? You really loved that umbrella, you don't remember it? You found it afterwards in your dressing room in the theater, but the spring was broken, and you said: Somebody broke the spring, who was playing with the spring?

Carmella didn't answer now either, and he went on, leaning toward her, his voice became almost sweetish—Honest, that's what you said, that it reminded you of a parasol. He laughed, as if some shining *idée-fixe* had penetrated his brain. You remember it? You don't remember it? he said. Afterwards I bought you a red nylon umbrella, but you said you hated nylon, especially red, and you gave it to your sister, she'd always appear with the red umbrella. He chuckled. And you said: How pretty the red umbrella is on you. His face became shrouded and he chuckled aloud a moment. Honest, I'm talking nonsense, he said.

Carmella didn't answer now either, but her face was odd, turned aside, with the small nervous movements of her head. It was wet, her face, as if she was soaked to the skin now, too, as if she were walking home in the rain without an umbrella now, too, and I thought: Where is she looking? No, not at Dov is she looking, where is she looking like that, what is she seeing? It was hard for me to look at her and I returned to the sea that took on an indigo color, her head nodding in front of me above the indigo as if it was hard to hold itself on the neck, and something in her face reminded me of how she looked in the period after

Itamar's death, but I didn't know what. Suddenly I remembered that I had once read that the shore rejects foreign materials, but the human body is smart, I read, it has smart limbs, you can implant a titanium bone in the limbs, there's a replacement for the bones when they break or atrophy and you can implant metal, there are companies that specialize in coating metals, it just depends on the layer of coating, the precise cutting, but remembering and forgetting, what happens to remembering and forgetting? My scarf, my blue scarf, shouted the woman at the table in back, suddenly my blue scarf flew off, you don't see that my blue scarf flew off, catch it, you can't catch it, why don't you get up? But the man didn't get up and the scarf flew away to the shore hovering over the sand and going off to the sea. You never get up, said the woman, you don't care about anything, when it comes to me, you don't care about anything, and she stood slightly on tiptoe, but the scarf was now over the sea light and hovering like a paper snake, waving and flying on the waves blue on blue as if the blues couldn't be blended.

At the extreme corner of the street some street lamps were already turned on and there was an evening light, a light in which you see only the edges of things. But the café was strongly lighted.

As I said, it was twilight. The woman with the Doberman had left by now and so did the smoking girl, and now the man and the woman also left and the only one still sitting there was the man with the cello who said something to himself into the cello, and at the counter the waiter was sitting bent over some newspaper, probably solving other crossword puzzles. It started getting dark. On the promenade a couple walked hugging in the warm light of sunset, the lines crucified their bodies, and then a loaded furniture truck rumbled past, two dangling legs of a table wagging over the ledge as if any minute the table would fall, and on the sidewalk next to us a man slowly lumbered up with a wheelbarrow full of leaves, which in the light capering on the sea looked like a birdbath without birds. The leaves were nicely arranged and there were a few pine branches on them and some gravel to keep the leaves from flying off, but with every breeze, some tremor passed into the wheelbarrow, the leaf-birds moved with a kind of tempest of wings and the lumbering man bent over to tamp down the gravel, then he straightened his back, went on walking upright as a signpost with the wheelbarrow and the leaves clung to his shoulders and back, and

Carmella watched him. She sat leaning forward, sunk deep in the chair like a person who goes out to seek forgetting, but bent over like that, half lighted, she looked like a minified and shortened double of herself, and Dov was looking at her again with great concentration. His eyes sparkled close, almost squinting, and I thought: He's telling himself: A little more venom, a little more venom, please, he's telling himself: Where's the knife where's the needle of the syringe. I said to myself: Of course, he's preparing the syringe, he's got poison in the syringe, he's a doctor, he knows life, the arbitrary needle of life the impossibility of fixing things, knows the depth of the body and how little you see in x-rays how little you get to the root of the disease. But he suddenly became very gentle and very sad, brought his hand to his eyes and passed it over both eyes a moment as if he were banishing something standing before his eyes, then he went back to Carmella. You had a chignon then, it looked very beautiful on you the chignon, he said, his eyes fixed on the back of her neck didn't move from there for a long time, and again there was silence and only the sea was heard like a mighty noise of a choir. A glass café with a dance floor at the end of the street was now lit up all at once but nobody was dancing and there were no dances, and only a child stood there and a bird stood on his head and he raised his hand and patted the bird that didn't fly away. Dov held his face in both hands, his eyes still fixed on Carmella. Suddenly he said: We had a loquat tree in the window, remember the window? The loquats fell right into our window. He had a friendly voice suddenly, and Carmella turned around, one of her cheeks dropping down, as if it were stung, and I said to myself: Something's going on in her head, dammit, what's going on in her head, dammit. Something in her face reminded me again of how she looked in the period after Itamar's death, and that she said then how much he loved to be home, he always loved to stay home when she went to plays he always stayed home, and then Dov's voice reached me: Your second husband—his face changed all at once and he laughed again with obvious pleasure. You see, I've still got my title, I'm your first husband, you can't ignore that, he said again in the especially amiable voice. His face expanded, as if it were waking up, and he said: With your second husband did you also have long plays? Sometimes I'd go to those plays a few times, I always looked for your husband at the play, he stayed home, I understand, I never saw him at the play.

Carmella threw him the look he was surely waiting for, and he again made a quick little turn, looking at her from the side again with great concentration as if he were searching on her face her wild thoughts.

I understand that your sister sometimes lived with you then, too, you were always a good sister. His voice was dry now and he laughed.

There was silence. He waited, his silhouette moved softly on the chair. I understand that I had gotten on a train you can't get off of, he said.

Carmella didn't answer. Her eyes were burning, the eyes of a person gnawed by one single thought, but her jaws had dropped and she looked confused as if at that moment she was suffering an awful loss.

He again turned half his body on the chair. The thin strip of hair on the forehead dropped to the side, revealing the bare skull, and he raised it with a quick movement. Did you hit your hand? You've got a little bruise on your hand, he said. His look became veiled suddenly. That's ridiculous, I'm ridiculous, he said, and moved the chair away a little.

Carmella didn't answer now either, her eyes were staring into the distance at some fixed point and the pupil became small, almost a small black dot.

He moved the chair away a little more and looked at her silently, leaning back, as if his look came to her from two directions at the same time. Your innocent walk on the seashore, I just ruined your innocent walk on the seashore, I'm sorry, he said.

Carmella didn't answer now either, looking at that same distant fixed place, her pupils still small and shrunken, two small almost fixed black dots, and that was how she was when we went to her sister the next day, silent all the way as if she were mute. It was hot. The road was bustling. Traffic didn't move. We got stuck at lights and the trip took a long time. When we arrived her sister was standing and hanging up laundry, holding the clothespins in a plastic bag with one hand, and when she saw us, the bag fell down, and she bent over and carefully gathered up the clothespins, putting them back in the bag and tying it with a rubber band. What a surprise, she said admiringly, in this heat, in the afternoon, and she added quickly: Wait a minute, go inside and meanwhile, I'll finish hanging the laundry, and she really did follow us inside soon, trudging, apparently very tired. Really, what a surprise, she repeated exuberantly, and I'll make us coffee, but first some cold water, or maybe iced tea, I've got a full pitcher of iced tea ready, and we drank iced tea. Then she apologized for being in a bathrobe. How I must look, she said, and changed into a big flowered dress that exposed thin, flaccid arms. Such guests, in the middle of the day, I'm excited, honest, she repeated again and brought coffee with little cookies she had left over from the weekend, apologizing: I keep them sealed, and they stay crisp, really good, like they were just baked, and they really were crisp and good. It was a small house at the edge of the Moshava surrounded by a small garden, and the entrance was covered with an awning of vine branches with bunches of small fragrant grapes hanging on it. The room was airy and despite the heat, it felt pleasantly cool. You missed me all of a sudden, eh? she said and smiled at Carmella, believe me, I sometimes miss you too, but there's no time, always there's no time, and Carmella said: Yes, we were sitting the two of us in a café on the seashore and suddenly I told her that I once gave you a red umbrella, you remember it? Really? said her sister. Yes, my red umbrella, you don't remember my red umbrella? Honest, said her sister. Carmella fixed her with one of her penetrating looks and her sister said: What is it, did something happen? Why do you look like that, what happened? Carmella laughed, all the while keeping her eyes fixed on her sister. I told you, we were sitting in a café on the seashore, you know, it's nice to sit on the seashore. You could sense a slight swerve in her voice, still all the while keeping her eyes fixed on her sister, who said again: Something happened, honest, something happened, what happened? And she sat down on the sofa. Carmella laughed again. You keep the guitar, she said, looking at the guitar that was hanging over the sofa. Yes, said her sister, but I haven't touched it in years, I just dust it. She smiled at Carmella, then she smiled at me. Inside, it's full of dead moths, she said, its whole body, dead moths, and again she smiled at Carmella, then she smiled at me. It's really full of dead moths, she said and turned her head to the guitar. When I dust it I like to stroke the strings. I don't know why I don't do it, she said.

You loved the guitar so much, Carmella said.

Yes, loves, you know, said her sister. She shrugged slightly. That's life, you know, that's life, she said, and Carmella said: I understand, and tossed out something about the dresses with shoulder straps. Just imagine me today in dresses with shoulder straps, said her sister, and smiled her wandering smile again. Meanwhile, we finished the coffee, and a few bunches of ripe grapes came and we ate grapes. The conversation was carried on in slow motion. Carmella distractedly swallowed the small sweet grapes, staring now and then at the floor as if some hole in the floor were gaping open, and suddenly she got up and said we should go back early, otherwise we'd get stuck again and again in some traffic jam and wouldn't get out of it, and the sister said: That's right, you're right, it's awful, but first eat something, I've got trout with wine and almonds, it's excellent, honest, you know that I'm an expert with trout, but Carmella said: Fine, next time, and again she said something about the traffic jam, and we returned on the old bypass road. The road was empty and there was an even greater emptiness all around. A man in shorts was jogging with small steps and on the balcony of a solitary house stood a girl. Carmella turned on the radio. Then she turned off the radio. She said: Her trout with wine and almonds is excellent, we could have stayed and eaten something, you're not hungry? Of course I said I wasn't hungry. Her face capered in silent laughter and she said: Yes, that's her specialty, trout with wine and almonds, when I used to come with Itamar she always made trout with wine and almonds, Itamar liked it very much, she said.

Meanwhile we had come to the long boulevard of palms. The light was strong. The boulevard burned in a green flame. You didn't hear the trees rustling but you saw them moving, the crests were swallowed up one after another in the flame, and Carmella said it was a good idea to travel on the bypass, and she loved that boulevard, with Itamar they'd always go back through that boulevard. Only in the summer, the dust, the next time maybe we'd go in the winter, she said, and I said: Fine, we'll go in the winter. She asked what in the winter. I said: Nothing, you mentioned winter. Yes, really, I don't know, she said. Then she said: Itamar died in the winter. Her face became small all at once. And he did love winter very much, she said. Something was seen coming close and then was seen going away. She bent forward and clutched the steering wheel. What a hard steering wheel, she said and slowed down a little, then she stepped on the gas and started dashing down the empty road.

At the next intersection, she got off the road and leaned her head on the steering wheel. Then she lifted it slightly. Did you hear what she said about the guitar? she said and returned to the road. My headache, and I've got a play tonight, I don't know how I'll go on stage, she said, moving her head to one side and then to the other side as if she had dead areas before her eyes. But you know, the show must go on, she said.

The jogger was already returning now, running with those small quick steps, red and drenched with sweat, and her face again capered with that same silent laugh. You see, he's running, running, she said.

Translated by Barbara Harshav